COIN

Ed Adams

First published in Great Britain in 2020 by firstelement

Directed by thesixtwenty

10 9 8 7 6 5 4 3 2

A CIP catalogue record for this book is available from the British Library.

ISBN 13 : 978-1-9163383-0-2
Ebook ISBN : 978-1-9163383-1-9

Printed and bound in Great Britain by Ingram Spark

rashbre
an imprint of firstelement.co.uk
rashbre@mac.com

ed-adams.net

To Julie and Melanie

THANKS

A big thank you for the tolerance and bemused support from all of those around me. To John, for the proofing, Georgina for artistic suggestions, to the lads from West Hatch for cover down-selection and curry. To thesixtwenty.co.uk for direction.

Barry and Steph for positive vibes and taking away the crates. To the NaNoWriMo gang for the continued inspiration and encouragement.

And, of course, thanks to the extensive support via the random scribbles of rashbre via http://rashbre2.blogspot.com and its cast of amazing and varied readers whether human, twittery, smoky, cool kats, photographic, dramatic, musical, anagrammed, globalized or simply maxed-out.

My blogging started in the days when the Electronic Frontier Foundation warned about the safe preservation of online identity; "Mind the Gap" as we Londoners say.

Nowadays it can be like the wild west out there. The difference is today's gold rush is digital.

Not forgetting the cast of characters involved in producing this; they all have virtual lives of their own.

And of course, to you, dear reader, for at least 'giving it a go'.

Books by Ed Adams include:

Triangle Trilogy		**About**
1	The Triangle	Dirty money? Here's how to clean it
2	The Square	Weapons of Mass Destruction – don't let them get on your nerves
3	The Circle	The desert is no place to get lost
4	The Ox Stunner	The Triangle Trilogy – thick enough to stun an ox
		(all feature Jake, Bigsy, Clare, Chuck Manners)
Archangel Collection		
1	Archangel	Sometimes I am necessary
2	Raven	An eye that sees all between darkness and light
3	Card Game	Throwing oil on a troubled market
4	Magazine Clip	the above three in one heavy book.
5	Play On, Christina Nott	Christina Nott, on Tour for the FSB
		(all feature Jake, Bigsy, Clare, Chuck Manners)
Stand-Alone Novels		
1	Coin	Get rich quick with Cybercash – just don't tell GCHQ
2	Pulse	Want more? Just stay away from the edge
3	Edge	Power can't be left to trust
4	Now the Science	the above three in one heavy book.
Blade's Edge Trilogy		
1	Edge	World end climate collapse and sham discovered during magnetite mining from Jupiter's moon Ganymede.
2	Edge Blue	A human outcome, after a doomsday reckoning, unless…
3	Edge Red	An artificially intelligent outcome, unless…

About Ed Adams Novels:

Triangle Trilogy		**About**
1	Triangle	Money laundering within an international setting.
2	Square	A viral nerve agent being shipped by terrorists and WMDs
3	Circle	In the Arizona deserts, with the Navajo; about missiles stolen from storage.
4	Ox Stunner	the above three in one heavy book.
		(all feature Jake, Bigsy, Clare, Chuck Manners)
Archangel Collection		
1	Archangel	Biographical adventures of Russian trained Archangel, who, as Christina Nott, threads her way through other Triangle novels.
2	Raven	Big business gone bad and being a freemason won't absolve you
3	Card Game	Raven Pt 2 – Russian oligarchs attempt to take control
4	Magazine Clip	the above three in one heavy book.
5	Play On, Christina Nott	Christina Nott, on Tour for the FSB
		(all feature Jake, Bigsy, Clare, Chuck Manners)
Now the Science Collection		
1	Coin	cyber cash manipulation by the Russian state.
2	Pulse	Sci-Fi dystopian blood management with nano-bots
3	Edge	World end climate collapse and sham discovered during magnetite mining from Jupiter's moon Ganymede
4	Now the Science	the above three in one heavy book.
Blade's Edge Trilogy		
1	Edge	World end climate collapse and sham discovered during magnetite mining from Jupiter's moon Ganymede.
2	Edge Blue	Endgame, for Earth – unless?
3	Edge Red	Museum Earth – unless?

Table of Contents

PART ONE

Going a Bomb

Almost pedantically, she added: "They're not really bombs--
they're acoustic provocations."
— J.G. Ballard, Millennium People

Red Alert

"Look around for a Bomb; we're on Red Alert," the security guard poked his head into the small room where Tyler was working. The guard's handheld radio was bleeping and squawking.

"Just have a look for anything suspicious in here, please," continued the guard as he moved away.

Tyler could not believe it. He had not been in this post for long, and already something like this was happening. The scrappy room Tyler was in was full of faded brown cardboard boxes. He had only been using the room because he needed access to a lumbering, specialised piece of equipment. He needed to use an old deep transcription device to check some materials.

Now Tyler was stuck in the middle of a messy room with instructions to poke and pry around in case the room contained something dangerous. Tyler decided that this was not a very likely target. The room was in a basement and was quite close to one of the main entrances to the building. There was a man on the door supported with the usual paraphernalia of access controls.

Someone would need to get past the entire system and then place whatever it was in a pretty improbable location, where it might emit a muffled thud.

No. It would not be here.

It was an old building, close to a busy main road with a slight patina of low-level dust over much of the content of the room. Nothing too obvious, but you could tell that this was a building that did not have the latest in air conditioning or other environmental control systems — a civil servants' building with a history.

Tyler decided it was time to have a break from his task. Not the bomb search, but the original reason he'd gone to the room. Maybe it would be even better to take an early lunch break.

The Piccolo, a small Italian sandwich bar across the road, beckoned and he thought to himself that he was so much closer to lunch from this basement room than right the way back to his third-floor office.

Tyler placed the materials into one of the drawers in the desk of the transcription unit. He could head back to ground level and straight out through the security doors. A cheese submarine was luring him, and the transcription could wait.

Submarine, Torpedo; those Italians had it nailed long before Subway arrived.

Outside, autumn, busy London streets and traffic moving oblivious to the excitement in the adjacent building.

Tyler turned right out of the building, walked about a hundred yards and then turned right again towards the Italian snack bar.

They had some of the best sandwiches and rolls in the area. Maybe something with mozzarella cheese? Or chorizo with brie? Suddenly, a crack sound and low-frequency thunder. Tyler thought it sounded like a truck had run into a wall. He noticed a group of starlings and pigeons flutter up from a nearby courtyard.

Then he heard a couple of car alarms bleeping although rumble of traffic from the main street continued uninterrupted.

Tyler heard the first of the sirens; they sounded as if they were moving along Cheapside. He figured it had been an explosion, but it seemed to be further west than his office.

No hoax, then, but where had it been targeted?

Tyler thought the Department was nothing like he expected. C-SOC. Cyber Security Operations Centre. It was almost an accident that he even got to be working there.

General office

Tyler's general office was a mix of styles. Being a government department meant it was subjected to normal cost-cutting and other types of economies. For example, it acquired random items of furniture to augment the office space.

There was a skeleton set of metal desks with side cabinets. These were in a kind of battleship grey colour. Around the edges of the room were a range of further grey steel cabinets each lockable and including a combination arrangement with pushbuttons. Such security was a casual deterrent, but it would be relatively easy to cut through a thin pin at the hinge where the door was held in place by the locking mechanism. It seemed absurd that a security office would be so lax.

The desks included various shelving systems dated from the 1980s through to modern times. There were some made of a kind of yellowish shiny wood, and the most modern ones had cable ducting included in amongst the stainless steel and plastic fitments of the units.

Tyler's desk was typical and was in a small configuration of four desk units arranged in a rectangle. Everyone had organised a barricade along the top of their desks. It meant that they were socially screened from their nearest neighbours.

Tyler's bosses' name was Marcus, and he was a few years older than Tyler. He had also started working in the Department direct from University. He wore a jacket most days and looked several years older than his real age, maybe because of his choice of spectacles. Opposite Tyler sat Rosie, who was around the same age as Marcus and also a mathematician but with a specialist interest in Artificial Intelligence. After Marcus, Rosie looked positively young, and Tyler would have placed her around his age until she spoke with such authority.

Tyler was pretty sure that he was a lightweight compared with those two in terms of general knowledge and experience, although Tyler had noticed that most of the mathematics was not especially complicated, mainly if one had access to computing power to help.

Tyler could see that Marcus had ingrained himself in the ways of the Department and also the type of global events that could trip instabilities. Marcus was a security analyst's analyst. His knowledge of unusual world events was vast, and he seemed to have high perception and an ability to link events together.

Rosie provided a kind of yang to Marcus's yin. She would often ask smart questions that probed into an event or situation, and then Marcus would pause, consider and as often as not respond with theory.

Tyler knew it would take him ages to find a similar degree of command over the role.

Instead, he made do pawing through the enormous amount of paper that everyone seemed to have on their desks.

In a modern world, Tyler had expected more to be electronic using the computer systems. It soon became apparent that it was mostly a question of timing.

The Department was given things to process that had been obtained by dubious means and were often physical rather than electronic. There was a big department somewhere out in Gloucestershire where items were sent to get them converted into electronic format.

However, there was a problem with this; it meant that the material would be encoded, but this could mean that sometimes essential things were missed.

At its simplest, it could be that the handwritten scribbles on a paper were not visible. In a more clandestine world, it could mean that something else on the physical document would not be noticed such as a small embedded chip or even a microdot.

It didn't end with paper, Tyler's team and the surrounding teams also received CDs, DVDs, memory sticks, physical tape in various formats (even some punched paper tape to process on one occasion).

It did feel a bit like sifting through someone's rubbish bin on occasions, and some of the material already looked as if it had been in a rubbish bin before selection.

The timing aspect was quite important because it would mean that most of the material received was fresh rather than having been on a round trip to the middle of Britain before the teams were able to examine it.

Tyler could also see from the material written in 'clear' on most of the documents that they were often targeting high profile individuals who connected with government or other public figures.

Perhaps considered snooping, the official line was that it was providing security services for the United Kingdom. As a consequence, the Department linked to other well-known and higher profile government departments.

Tyler and Matt

Years earlier, at university, Tyler was one of the bright ones.

He was involved with mathematics projects that obliquely had something to do with gambling. He had tried his theory in practice and come unstuck.

He'd dug himself a financial hole. He shared the flat with two other people, one of whom was Matt, a Masters student who everyone regarded as something of a Brainiac. He, Matt and Kyle had come up with a scheme, created mainly by Matt, to fund their lifestyle.

Matt was far ahead of Tyler in his exploitation of computers to get to the results he'd need. He'd sit in his room, with Tom Waits blasting on the stereo and write complex algorithms designed to provide ever-increasing security around whatever he was doing.

Tyler's research into gambling game theory meant he had stumbled across the systems used to secure the money used in online gambling. The whole environment was locked down, and normal currency used only to get initial access into the systems. The cyber currency was used for betting because it made the whole process more secure.

Even the national lottery operated this way, requiring the punters to preload money converted into e-cash before they could place their bets.

In his flat, he'd first asked Matt about cybercash and then worked with him on various attempts at get-rich-quick schemes. He ran the gambling and Matt calculated odds. Neither of them was particularly successful, although Tyler had lost the most money.

Kyle was mostly the onlooker. He was also smart but had branched out into quantum physics, with the kind of maths that the others thought was taking liberties.

One evening they were sharing a pizza.

"There's a way to mine for the keys to crypto-currency," said Matt, pulling at the tear-and-share garlic bread.

"But aren't they controlled by big business?" asked Tyler.

"More likely by organised crime," answered Kyle, "And there are so many keys required to support the ever-increasing amount of currency required."

Matt nodded towards his room in the flat.

"I've invested in a cyber currency miner," he announced, "I've used my student loan."

Tyler looked surprised. Kyle nodded, "I knew it! I knew you were up to something!"

Matt responded, "Tyler, don't look at me like that. You've spent your loan on gambling, I've spent mine on an investment."

The three of them laughed. All knew they were on the edge of dealing with something shady.

"C'mon then, show me," said Tyler, as he grabbed a slice of pepperoni pizza.

Matt unlocked his room. A small metal frame was standing on the desk. It whirred quietly, and the others could make out the row of small electric fans underneath what looked like a row of computer innards.

Any sounds from the computer were drowned by Matt playing a noisy CD.

"Tom Waits, Rain Dogs, you like?" smiled Matt.

The others chuckled, it was always Tom Waits with Matt.

"Okay, this is it," said Matt, pitting to the desk, "It's a multi-processor set up solely to look for cryptographic data."

"Did you make it?" asked Tyler, noticing the somewhat bare-bones nature of the device.

"No," answered Matt, "I bought it online. It is specialist gear. Its only job is to look for blockchains that can validate cryptocurrency. I get paid for each one I find."

"Blockchains?" asked Tyler.

"Yes, Blockchains; the mathematically certified blocks of information that chain cybercurrency transactions together and confirm their validity."

"And is it worth it?" asked Tyler, "How much do you get paid for finding these blockchains?"

"Well, it's new, but I should get at least £200 per month from this rig if I follow the user instructions."

"So how long to repay for the equipment?"

"Six months at that rate and I've already deducted the cost of the power – which works out to around £3 per day, to use the setup. And…"

Matt could hardly contain himself.

"...I've worked out that I can also acquire direct cyber currency from this system. You know I said user instructions, well, we all know what the manual is for, don't we?"

"Except when building flat-pack furniture, when it can be quite useful," chipped in Kyle.

"That's right, and you know, the cyber currency is worth significantly more than the blockchains that I'm supposed to search for."

Tyler nodded. He knew, from his attempts at get-rich-quick, that cyber currency was worth significant cash if channelled effectively.

"By being creative with the instructions, I've created three cyber coins," said Matt, "They're worth a lot. I tweaked the algorithms – reprogrammed the system - the whole rig is configurable."

"How much?" asked Kyle, "Those cyber coins are quite valuable."

"Yes, they are, it's around £9,000. The coins are worth around £3k each, based on the currency exchange."

"£9,000 Not bad, eh?"

"So how are you playing this?" asked Kyle. "If you tell too many people, won't they all come looking for a payout?"

"Not really," said Matt," I've only told you two so far, and that's because I want to see whether you'd be interested in coming in with me. It takes a gambling mentality to make this all work."

Tyler was taken aback, "Wow, this is a lot to take in. Why would you want us to help, and what would be my part of the bargain?"

"It's okay; I've been thinking about this for a while. We're all good at maths; we want to make money; we don't mind taking risks. I can handle the background technology, as long as you can think about the best ways to stash the currency. By that I mean we'll need to pass it into the main systems via gambling web sites and then cash it in through their payout sites. I want to set up a holding company into which I'll funnel the clean money."

"You, Tyler, have already got the gambling profile. As we feed the cybercash into the system, it will just look as if you have had a turn of luck. Then we can cash it in through one of the banking systems."

"So, ...laundering the money?" asked Kyle.

"Kind of...I just don't want to draw attention to the way we are discovering it. Nor the volume. Much easier to look like an addicted gambling punter is feeding it in."

Matt looked at Tyler and they both grinned. Kyle looked less enthusiastic.

"Shake?" said Tyler. "Sure" said Matt.

"I may give this one a miss," said Kyle, "It's a little too close to the edge for me. But what's in this room stays here."

"Like Fight Club?" asked Tyler.

"What's Fight Club?" answered both Matt and Kyle simultaneously.

Tyler and Matt knew Kyle could be relied upon to keep the secret. They also knew he was probably the smartest of the three of them.

"Okay, but Tyler," said Matt, "First of all, I'll need you to do something for me...You need to meet some people."

Job Offer

Matt gave Tyler an invitation to a meeting at a fancy London hotel.

"I want you to go as the representative of our agreement. I don't want to go because they could ask me direct questions. If they ask you, you won't know the answers. No offence."

"It's not the first time," Tyler grinned.

"Anyway, it should be fun, enjoy a cocktail or two!"

Tyler went along, at least to sample the fineries offered by the hotel. There he met a couple of computer specialists from a government department, which later turned out to be the one that would employ both him and Matt.

The representatives already knew about Matt, and it made Tyler wonder if they were in some way monitoring Matt's computer work. At the time, Tyler thought there was something that he or Matt had done which somehow broke the law.

Instead, they offered to double the fees from the cyber coins that Matt discovered, if Matt and Tyler would sign up with them for a couple of years of work at the end of their studies. The offer amounted to pretty easy money, and they gave Tyler a chance to talk it over with Matt before agreeing.

The organisation would match their original gains like-for-like, as a signing-on fee and if Matt and Tyler discovered more keys or cyber coins, they would get even more money.

Tyler discussed this with Matt, and they were both 'in'.

This scheme worked pretty well until Tyler discovered Erica's long legs, which put the project onto the back burner.

By that time, Matt had found some more keys, so altogether they were turning a tidy profit from the cyber coins, match-funded and tax-free.

That was when Tyler had his European self-discovery adventure with Erica.

Upon their return, Tyler received his degree and the job offer from the government department. Erica had a job waiting for her in finance. Tyler would be in the same government unit as Matt, although their roles would be different. They ended up on different teams, and after Tyler moved into a flat with Erica, he hardly saw Matt.

Tyler had expected his work to be about cryptography or something that related to the type of math he had been doing at University.

Instead, it was surprisingly well-paid paper shifting and was how he now found himself strolling along St Martin-le-Grand eating a mozzarella sub.

Making sense of it

"Whenever you become anxious or stressed, outer purpose has taken over, and you lost sight of your inner purpose.

You have forgotten that your state of consciousness is primary, all else secondary."

—*Eckhart Tolle, A New Earth: Awakening to Your Life's Purpose*

Towards or away?

Tyler had stuffed the remains of his lunch into a pocket. In the distance, he could see a small plume of smoke. He retraced his steps towards Cheapside, from where he would be able to get a better line of sight towards the direction of the commotion.

It took him about two minutes to walk to the main road, and as he did, he could see several police cars and ambulances noisily cutting through the traffic and heading towards the west.

Then, turning onto the busy Cheapside, he could see the source of the commotion. Previously, obscured by the tall buildings ha now had a better view. Tyler looked up at the buildings wondering if there would be broken panes of glass or other tell-tale signs. Everything else looked normal. There didn't even seem to be much interest from the adjacent buildings as he estimated that the explosion was probably two hundred metres away.

Far enough to mean that people inside the buildings had not been directly affected except maybe to hear a loud bang which could be mistaken for any number of London street sounds. Tyler was more aware because of the alert that had already sounded in his secure and slightly privileged environment. Now the question was whether he should go closer to the action or slide quietly back into the office.

Well, what else could he do? He decided to visit the action and see what had happened.

"After all," he reasoned, "It's not every day that a major news incident occurs close by," let alone in his lunch break.

Tyler walked further along the road towards the area that had the early signs of being cordoned. As he approached, he realised that this was not an academic situation but that there were likely to be real people involved in the catastrophe. There was a confusion of people as he reached the outer perimeter established by the police.

They were using blue and white tape stretched across the road and improvising a diversion away from the whole zone. Tyler could see a few people walking towards him with dust on their clothing and realised that they were speaking French. Most people were making a space for those leaving the area to get away quickly.

"You don't want to go down there," said one of the people passing, "It was some kind of car bomb."

Tyler checked his phone to see if there was any further information.

"Reports are just coming in…" said the first report.

The situation was still very new, and news crews didn't seem to have got their reporting teams on-site.

Tyler's training told him to be aware that there could sometimes be a second explosion, and perhaps it was better to stay back. One of the policemen was turning people away. He was saying that there was nothing for anyone to see.

"It's more important that we can get the emergency services in and out of here quickly," the policeman said. "We don't want all of you acting as an additional roadblock."

Tyler could see a black-windowed American-style van leaving the scene. He assumed it was one of the London-based rapid-response specialist units and that they would be all over the situation in a few more minutes,

As he looked towards the damaged area, he tried to work out which building had been involved. He didn't recognise it at all.

Tyler took a couple of pictures on his phone and turned around. The explosion was going to be the biggest story on the television and media tonight.

As Tyler walked back toward the office, he knew that the Department would be in trouble over the event. The Department should have detected the threat in some way, especially when it was so close to home.

Tyler thought that he was low down enough in the pecking order, such that he should not suffer any direct repercussions.

He decided that a small amount of road dust on his face might be appropriate as he walked back into the building. It would give him additional plausibility when the inevitable department meeting was called.

As Tyler returned to the building and climbed the stone steps at the side entrance, he noticed that the doors were locked.

There was a sign which requested he go around to the main entrance lobby which was on another street.

He noticed his boss and several others caught out in the same way and muttering under their breaths as they made the way the extra 300 yards to the other side of the building and up another set of steps to the larger main lobby which was also used by visitors. It was evident that they were putting in place a new secure process as they tried to get back into the building.

Tyler couldn't help but think about horses, stables and bolts as everyone went through this new process. He had to swipe and then show his badge to the usual guy. Then he had to do the sort of thing usually reserved for visitors and which involved putting possessions through the airport-style scanning system.

Eventually, Tyler was reunited with his badge, loose coins and phone. Tyler was faintly amused at the way that these old buildings were adapted for this high-tech security. There was even one where the scanner looked like it was made of wood instead of the usual high-tech frontage. Tyler knew it was inevitable that there would be a departmental meeting and that there was a pretty high chance it had already started.

He made his way to his office and there spotted a large group already huddled in the big meeting room.

Department

Tyler walked into the department meeting. He was not the only person to be late. His boss, Marcus, was also delayed. Tyler decided it was easiest to join with Marcus and probably give the impression that they had been somewhere together. There were a few chairs still at the front, so Tyler and Marcus sat down next to one another.

The overall head of the unit, Jim Cavendish, was already talking "... Extra vigilance in these troubled times," he was saying. Tyler thought he could probably have written the first part of his speech."

The piece Tyler would have difficulty to predict was the sheer amount of new procedure to be added as a consequence of the bomb attack.

Tyler had seen those "what to do if someone rings with a bomb threat" notices and attended the vigilance course. He had also completed the two courses about anti-terrorism and threat management processes. He'd got the certificates from both of them, based upon the little tests that they made him do at the end.

"... Details of the attack are still scarce," Jim continued.

"There is still uncertainty of where the attack was delivered because there is a news blackout on the area."

Tyler raised his hand. He had not planned to, but as he knew more about this from first-hand viewing, he thought it would be something he should mention. Jim looked toward him. Tyler could tell Jim could not remember his name. Then he looked toward Marcus, "Marcus, does your team have something to add to this?"

Marcus looked at Tyler. He realised that he didn't know anything about what Tyler had seen and would be unable to deduce it from Tyler's expression. Tyler squinted his eyes first towards Marcus and then to Jim Cavendish.

"Yes," Tyler found himself saying, "I did see the immediate aftermath of the explosion along by Warwick Lane. I was there a few minutes after it happened. There was already a police cordon in operation, and they were letting people out of the area but not letting people back in."

"As well as the police, ambulances and fire brigade, I could see an RRT around the scene within the first few minutes. I was far enough away to only really be able to see the evacuees from the situation who all looked quite shaken up. "

At this point, Tyler remembered that he had added some minor dust to his clothing as part of his potential excuse when he returned to the office.

Tyler brushed his shoulder for effect and was pleased to see a small amount of dust rise into the air.

Tyler brushed his sleeves, and there was a further convincing amount of dust, so he continued, "The whole area was covered in dust as a result of the explosion. At this time, we can only guess what caused it, but I overheard people from the scene saying it was a car bomb."

Lord Raglan

"Thank you," said Jim. "... Thank you, Marcus, and your team for that update."

Tyler could see that Marcus looked pleased about this but suspected that he would also be irritated that Tyler had not managed to tell him about it before we got into the meeting.

"Does anyone else have any information about this?" continued Jim.

There was silence. The people looked around, and Tyler was aware most people seemed to look at him.

Jim continued, but it was more of the corporate waffle about extra vigilance.

Tyler thought that the whole meeting hadn't said much. It was all based upon somewhat limited information: Yes - there's been a bomb. Yes - there's been a bomb threat and then an explosion. Yes - it has targeted something which we believe to be one of our other buildings, but that's all anyone knew.

Tyler knew slightly more just because he visited the area.

The other side of the meeting room was a flat-screen monitor. It was generally used for PowerPoint presentations, and Tyler asked, "So I wonder if the television will show us any other information? We could tune into the news channel."

Jim looked towards the television.

"Can someone switch it on?" he asked.

There was the usual meeting room array of buttons and switches, but as usual, no one knew how to get normal television pictures on the monitor.

Eventually, somebody from the IT department stepped forward and pressed a few buttons. It looked like the screen needed to reboot itself before it could be used as an ordinary television, but it soon had a picture from the main news feeds which showed the scene very much as Tyler had seen it a few minutes before.

TV crews had managed to use long lenses to get better access to the source of the explosion. It appeared a car or van was used to bomb the front of the building.

The building looked only lightly damaged although there were broken glass and fragments strewn around.

It looked as if the blast had mainly been deflected upwards rather than at the building itself. A news reporter was saying something repetitively about the explosion. It was evident that there was very little new information available. The reporter continued, "it looks as if there is a news blackout on this whole situation."

Tyler looked across to where Rosie was sitting. He raised his eyebrows and shook his left hand in a gesture. It was a "shall we go for a pint?" gesture.

Rosie nodded and also lightly tapped Marcus on the arm. The three would go out for a drink in a nearby pub. They could talk about this more expansively away from the office.

Jim's meeting was coming to a close. It broadly said everyone should expect there to be more paperwork and admin to support the increased level of security.

Tyler and his mini-team moved across to the Lord Raglan. It was a typical old-school London boozer. Handily positioned for the city folk to be able to grab a pint after work and it still had the old city tradition of closing early at 9 PM. However, it was open for most of the day and was something of an extra office for a few of the staff.

They stood at the bar around the corner from the main serving area.

"What do you reckon?" asked Rosie.

"What, of Jimbo's pitch? I don't think he knew that much," answered Tyler.

Jimbo had become the nickname for Jim Cavendish, acquired in the distant past and passed from team to team. Although new, Tyler knew he had the right to use Jim's nickname when talking to colleagues.

"Is it a random or the start of a campaign?" continued Rosie.

"It's more than bang and burn. Whoever it is seems to be targeting us," said Marcus, "At least it's government departments at any rate. I don't think there's anything to suggest that other people are being targeted at the moment."

"Where did the original alert come from?" asked Rosie.

"I don't know," said Marcus, "but it looks as if they have a more than working knowledge of our setup."

"Either that or they've just been able to use our systems against us," Tyler said.

"If they know how to get a message about this into the system, then we will inevitably disperse it to all of the offices. All they need to do is have one location, and the rest will follow."

"Yes," said Rosie,

"And if you're right they've hit one of the smaller offices, which could be easier to gain access to than the bigger Department buildings."

"I still can't believe how we've allowed ourselves to grow in this topsy-turvy manner," said Marcus.

"You'd think we'd all be in a campus environment where there could be a proper security cordon."

"Yes," said Rosie,

"The problem is it would then need to be somewhere out of town, and then they'd have a problem getting the right people to the resource it.

"Yes," Tyler added,

"It's easier to recruit people into the centre of London, and when we need people with special languages or other skill sets, they are easier to obtain."

"That's the point," said Marcus,

"As we casually obtain specialists for certain roles, they could themselves be a new source of the problem."

"What?" Said Rosie, "with all of the positive vetting that we do nowadays, I'd have thought that particular problem was over,"

"I'm not so sure," Tyler said, "The more people we have involved with this, the more likelihood there is that there will be an information leak."

"It must be pretty obvious to most people that unless we have all of our offices with names like Acme import-export that there will be areas that people find and exploit. But, in this case, if they manage to park a car or van outside the office block, then it doesn't bode well for resilience to future attacks."

"You wait," said Marcus, "I bet tonight they reintroduce the ring of steel or something similar around the city."

Marcus looked at both of us.

"There's going to be a task force, you know?" he said.

"I was called to another meeting before the Department's big one today. Several of the head of teams were asked to go along. We've been asked to be part of the task force."

Rosie smirked.

"Oh yeah, of all the people in London they select us three to be in the task force for the bombs?"

"Not exactly," said Marcus.

"We are just one of the teams asked to do this. The others in the meeting were to report to Nasreen and Janice. So, it will be all three of our teams, but don't assume that we are the only people involved."

Rosie chuckled.

"I can see that we would be the powerhouse needed to solve this mysterious crime!" she said.

"That's right," said Marcus. "They are getting people from all over the place involved with this. Our Department had to put some people up. Janice will be leading this and says Nasreen is going to have her team to do most of the analytics work. We are the third team."

Rosie grinned. "So, we are the gophers for this then?"

Tyler's phone rang.

"Hi, Tyler here...What...No," Tyler looked ashen.

"It's about Matt; he was a casualty in the first bomb. They are saying his body was found in the rubble. He's dead!"

"Do you need a few minutes?" asked Marcus, seeing the look on Tyler's face. Rosie had stood up as if to comfort Tyler.

"Yeah, maybe a short step outside," Rosie and Marcus nodded as Tyler stepped out of the pub into the street.

Rosie and Marcus made muted small talk while Tyler was outside.

Eventually, Tyler reappeared through the door of the Lord Raglan. He had been gone for about 15 minutes.

"Condolences", said Marcus quietly," I know you guys were good friends."

Rosie nodded. She still looked as if she wanted to hug Tyler, but Tyler's moves were quite spiky and forced as he sat down to resume his pint.

"This is all wrong," said Tyler, "I don't even know why Matt would be at that building."

They paused, and each looked into their drink.

Marcus picked up the conversation again.

"It's all the more important that we sort this thing out. I'll try to tell you what I know."

"And remember when Nasreen's team or Janet's team need something done, we are their go-to people."

Rosie laughed. "All three of us? I can see we will get a lot done with just three of us to do the work."

"I expect it will change quite quickly," said Marcus,

"They probably need to get the first team together fast, and that's why we've been chosen. We've all got the security clearances and know how everything works. I reckon that if this goes on for more than a week or two there will be a whole load of extra people added. That's not to mention the people over in Cheltenham and across the river, plus the usual police, et cetera."

Rosie added "Wow- this is something of a major gear shift from sifting through lots of paper. Instead of the usual work, we are suddenly onto a major case. And this has all happened within hours of the explosion along the road."

Tyler asked, "So, are we starting straight away?"

"Yes, right now in fact," said Marcus.

"I brought you here to tell you I expect Nasreen and Janice are doing something similar with their teams. There's going to be a new area of the building set aside for this."

"I hope it won't be in the basement near to one of the entrances," Tyler said.

"Although, I thought that the basement room that I was in for the bomb alert was probably one of the tougher parts of the building to gain entry to illicitly."

"We are starting in this building," said Marcus,

"But there's a pretty good chance that we will move so that we can start to join up with the other teams."

"However, it's likely to still be in central London because we'll need to be around where the probability of further attacks may be highest. "

"Is there much other intel on all of this?" asked Rosie.

"Yes," said Marcus.

"There's been a glut of information. I've seen it go across my desk but because we have been working on other programs it has not been high on our list up to this point."

Both Rosie and Tyler knew that there were often threats of one kind or another in circulation and part of the Department's job was also to filter out the noise from the real threats.

"Naturally this has gone to the very top of the pile now," Marcus added," This was inside the boundaries of the City of London, so it automatically gets a new high priority."

"We still don't know much about it though," Tyler said. "And although I was within eyesight of the scene, I still couldn't see very much."

"We've already got quite a lot more information than Jim was hinting at," said Marcus, "We needed to cover it up in the general briefing. Your little walk nearly blew the cover."

"Remember we got the threat, and also it hit one of our buildings. Despite what goes out in the press, there are video surveillance materials from the scene loaded to our systems."

The nook in the bar they were sitting in was empty.

"Where is everybody?" Tyler asked.

Rosie looked up from her drink.

"I had to hire this part of the pub for our meeting," said Marcus. "I'd arranged with the bar staff that they would close the area when we sat down. It's cost our department expenses a bit, but worth it," he added.

"Now, I need to know that both of you are fully engaged in this," said Marcus.

"Because if you are, then I will be issuing you both with new passes when we get back to the building," he added.

"I'm in," said Rosie, "This is the most interesting thing I've been involved with since I got here."

"Me too," Tyler added. He hadn't thought about this very much and decided that if both Marcus and Rosie thought this was a good thing, then he would undoubtedly be up for it as well.

At that stage, Tyler didn't particularly think about any downsides from involvement. Except for the obvious and fundamental one that his ex-flatmate had been blown up.

Time to move out

"It does not matter how long you are spending on the earth, how much money you have gathered or how much attention you have received.

It is the amount of positive vibration you have radiated in life that matters,"

—*Amit Ray, Meditation: Insights and Inspirations*

Backtrace and Level Up

The new office was about as unexceptional as Tyler had anticipated. The inner walls of the building had a curve to them, and the new room was a long, narrow and curved structure with tall glass windows along one side which looked out onto a grubby light well.

Tyler said he could not call it a courtyard because it was only about two or 3 metres wide. Rosie agreed. Across the other side was another room of a similar size although, mysteriously, the other one was a proper rectangle.

Tyler worked out that they were in an old machine room or storeroom.

It had desks and a phone and computer system but would be quite a grim place to spend the next few weeks.

"I suppose they could convert the whole building into a car-park, or something?" said Rosie.

The other teams were already in the room when Marcus's group arrived, and they had chosen the better desks.

It was marginal. The main advantage was that one end of the room was larger and lighter than the other and so the widest portion had been selected by the other two teams.

It also looked as if they'd cleared any unwanted items into the remaining space which did have four desks instead of three.

In all other respects, it was quite like the team's prior space. Except they were closer to their two compatriot teams.

The curved wall was already prepared as a pinboard that could be used to create timelines and various 'busy' pictures and charts to show progress.

Tyler marvelled at how much of what they were being asked to do was still manual rather than computerised.

The new workstations were wheeled in. The old kit they had used previously seemed to have received an instant upgrade to all the latest technology.

"Wow!" said Rosie. "At least we get some new gear out of this!"

"This new kit has to be highly secure as well," said Marcus.

"I know our normal stuff is pretty good, but this has extra capabilities to ensure it is secure. Don't try to tamper with the discs or anything," Marcus added, "Otherwise they will destruct."

One of the installers walked across to us. "That's right," he said, " In fact, these are perimeter security enabled as well. If you try to take any of this kit out of the building the disks will self-destruct."

"That could be interesting if we move to yet another building," said Rosie.

Marcus scheduled a special meeting for 5 pm.

Tyler was a little concerned about what time he would get away from the office. He reckoned the meeting might last for an hour and reached for his phone to call up his drinking buddies of the evening.

"I wouldn't bother with that," said Marcus.

"Your ordinary cell phone won't work in this space now. They've put up a microcell around here, and you will need one of the Department phones to make calls. The phones are encrypted but log everything, so we can keep track of what everyone in the team is doing."

"Civil liberties?" said Rosie.

"I think you'll find that this was something described in the paperwork you signed when we issued you with those new badges," said Marcus.

"Until this is over, you'll all be on silent running for everything to do with this operation."

One technician was walking around the office with a stack of boxes containing phones. They were all brand-new, and Tyler wondered whether they were charged so they could be used straight away. Eventually, they got to him and made him sign another set of paperwork.

"Here you are," said the phone technician, handing the phone across.

"It works just like a regular phone, but you can't add any new software, and it will record everything spoken. The tracking is also switched on permanently. It still looks like a normal phone so that you will not draw attention when you are out in public. You can still use your personal phone when you are out of the building as well," said the technician.

"Your regular phone is paired with this device and so it will also be monitoring what goes on with your normal phone."

"You should really only use this phone for any work calls now though."

"But if I want to play 'happy frog' I will need to use my own phone?" Tyler asked the technician. The woman from the telecoms department looked over. Tyler could tell she had heard every quip about phones before.

Tyler looked at the time on the new phone which showed 16:30. He was getting ready to correct it when he realised this was the real time. The drama of the day had made it pass very quickly. It was only half an hour until the meeting was due to start. A few minutes later a delivery of pizza arrived. Rosie stood up and moved to the middle of the room by the curved wall.

"Hello everyone. There's some pizza and some fizzy drinks. This is going to be a long evening."

At 5 o'clock Rosie provided a collated briefing about what had happened.

The alert about the bomb had arrived at around nine in the morning. The security services had not known what to make of it because it did not have any of the usual codewords or other authentication associated with typical bomb threats.

What it did have was substantial information about the locations used by the Department. It also named several of the people in the Department. For this reason, it escalated from a minor category to a top category threat by 11 o'clock. The threat had also indicated the timeframe for the explosion to be between 11:30 am and 12 o'clock.

Tyler was slightly surprised that the Department was able to respond so quickly. Most routine paperwork still took longer than this to move through the system, so this must have been expedited in some way.

It turned out that there had been a prior alert a day earlier that had signalled the intention of the bombers to send information on this morning.

Without any of them being aware, it had raised the alert level to Moderate and had put people in the monitoring areas on standby.

"So, what do we know about the original alert?" asked Tyler.

Rosie replied," It was challenging to work out where the alert originated. They transmitted it via an Internet phone call routed through about a dozen countries."

"The final apparent exchange it had come from was the headquarters of a large fizzy drinks manufacturer based in West London."

"The call had gone to a fire station in West London as well. The only code used was an internal code used by the fire service for signalling a high priority event."

"By the combination of routing and use of a fire station as an endpoint, the callers circumvented normal tracking systems, while still guaranteeing that the call was logged."

"For example, if they had called a police control centre or Whitehall office, then there would have been a backtrace available immediately on the call."

"The use of the fire station was clever because it was an emergency service. It would have a fast response, including access to other emergency hotlines. It was also somewhere largely considered operational rather than a specialist unit dedicated to any form of counterterrorism."

It was the first time that Rosie had used the word terrorism as she described this situation. Tyler wondered whether they were really involved with terrorists.

"The truth is, at the moment we don't know who is doing this nor why," said Rosie.

"Usually, when something like this happens, we get someone admitting to the incident almost immediately.

"This one is different. No one has admitted anything, and curiously even with this huge blast, there was only one fatality. Most of the explosion directed upwards resulting in property damage rather than multiple casualties.

Tyler leaned forward. "Only one fatality and that was my friend Matt?" he asked, "I don't like the sound of this."

Rosie continued, "After the explosion, the Met sent in a couple of drones to surface map the area quickly, and these are the results."

Rosie pressed a button on her phone, and nothing happened. She pressed the button again and still nothing happened.

Tyler realised that the team would need to get its act together to keep up with this. All of this technology required to work correctly. The idea of exploding disk drives and secret phones all seemed a bit of a step too far.

Rosie eventually showed the pictures. It was reminiscent of a missile attack. By the roadside were the charred remains of a van and a blast wall streaked up the side of a prominent stone building.

"See, it is amazing that the building withstood the blast. I think the reason the windows remained intact was that we have already bomb blast protected them."

Tyler asked," So this wasn't a regular civilian target then?"

"No", answered Marcus," This was one of our smaller offices handling quite sensitive information."

"How did Matt get hit then?" asked Tyler," It looks as if the blast was mainly external,"

"It was," said Rosie," Matt Stevens was outside the building at the time of the blast. Aside from him, only six people suffered minor injuries. It's almost as if the bomb was engineered to inflict the least damage."

"Okay, Marcus", said Rosie," You are going to have to level with us. There's more to these team choices than meets the eye."

"Alright", said Marcus," There are two things. Firstly, Tyler here knew Matt Stevens. As importantly, he knew Matt was working on blockchain uses."

Tyler shook his head," No. I was still a good buddy of Matt, but since we joined the Department, we've spent less time together than you might think. We don't share a flat any more, and I didn't even know he was working in the other building. And to be honest, Matt was far smarter than me when it came to cyber coins and the blockchains."

"What's the other thing?" asked Rosie, "You said there were two things."

"Yes. I'm wondering if was a warning? It ties into the cybercash work we did a few weeks ago based upon that Russia Today story," replied Marcus.

"What?" Said Rosie. "Those TV reports? Ones about Russian financial stability?"

"Yes, I wrote a report after that, which has gone through the reporting chain," said Marcus, "It implied that the Russians might have more to hide. Reports on Russia Today were talking up the rouble as if it was now one of the strongest currencies.

"In practice, the main strengthening of the currency is more the effect from its low base. Put simply, at the end of 2014 the dollar bought 56 roubles, then in 2015 it purchased 52, nowadays it's somewhere in the mid-40s."

"The rouble is bouncing back despite signs to the contrary. It is as if they have somehow found a mechanism to guarantee the price of the rouble," said Tyler.

Tyler nodded, "It's what Matt used to talk about. If there was a way to filter a cryptocurrency into a mainstream currency, then it could be used as a mini printing press to manufacture banknotes. And it would be almost undetectable."

"It would unhook the Russian oil dependency," said Rosie, "Instead of needing to sell oil, they could just turn up the speed of printing of currency."

"Yes," said Marcus, "but it would be better still for the Russians if they were able to generate a foreign currency - then it's much like the way they get foreign money from oil sales."

"What, instead of printing roubles, attempt to print the dollar or the euro or the pound?" asked Rosie.

"Precisely, if they can augment their supplies of foreign exchange. Quietly create the equivalence of dollars or euros," said Marcus.

"That's like a double-dip into the barrel," said Tyler. "On the one hand, the Russians could manipulate the oil price, and at the same time have an inflow of dollars or other hard currencies to provide themselves with a safety cushion."

"More than a cushion," said Rosie," It's a whole sofa."

"Yes," said Tyler. "That's what Matt used to get excited about. We only looked at the relative strengths of the various currencies with regard to selling our cryptocurrency. As students we just wanted to make a fast buck. And heck, the UK government were also kindly offering us double for our trouble."

"That's right," said Marcus, "You might not have realised it, but the system that Matt had developed was a great proxy for the status of all cryptocurrencies. We were buying into your data stream. The simplest way was to pay you both and, in return, get access to your data knowledge."

Tyler smiled, "Too good to be true. It's what we both thought, although we could not see your angle on it, we were happy to take the money."

Marcus nodded, "Yes, that is what I put into my report. Since the rouble began strengthening, it was at around the same time that oil prices began to rise again.

"My report said that it was such a short period that it wouldn't provide any real evidence that the rouble was capable of fighting against the low price of oil for any significant time. That's without even taking into effect account the effect of speculators. Imagine an exchange rate that mysteriously improves and yet no one is speculating on it. That can't last for very long!"

"So, Russia isn't banking on the strength of its own currency?" asked Tyler.

"Correct," said Marcus, "I suspect it is building reserves of foreign exchange, by bolstering them with laundered cyber coins."

"And all the while it is manipulating the availability of oil," added Rosie, "and it doesn't care about the effects that it is having on the rouble, because it has a secret stash of Forex."

"How come I haven't seen any of these reports from our direct team?" asked Tyler.

"Oh, you have," answered Marcus, "It's just not spelled out in such detail. It takes a whole set of events to allow us to draw these conclusions. I filed the paper about rouble manipulation some time ago, and to be honest there were several other people with similar conclusions. We couldn't predict the cyber coin implications, though."

Marcus nodded, "At least, that's what I said in my report. It was along the lines that with a cheap rouble that was stable, it was in Russia's interests to feed the speculators and encourage them by giving out cheap credit, thereby maintaining high interest rates.

"They couldn't do this for very long, though, because it would eventually stretch their own Central Bank and they would need to beef up the depleted foreign currency reserves. The irony is they would effectively have to bet against their own currency by buying foreign currency.

"I'm pretty sure there were lots of other people that made the same assumptions. In fact, I was taken to one side after that and asked to treat the whole thread of information as Protocol 6.

Tyler asked, "Protocol 6, it sounds like something from spy world?"

"Protocol 6 is like "Top Secret" - we use it to limit the number of people involved in a particular discussion," said Rosie.

"I notice that our new badges are protocol 6, so I kind of thought we'd made it to the next level. Like in some platform game," said Tyler.

"That's right," said Marcus, "and Tyler, you'll have gone through eDV checks to be in this role anyway."

"Oh, Mr Holmes, I would love to tell you, but then, of course, I'd have to kill you," chuckled Tyler.

Marcus continued, "It wasn't just the oil rouble pricing that I noticed, but it was a subsequent newsflash about a Russian drone filming oil wells that crash-landed in Saudi Arabia."

Marcus continued, "First of all, the Russians are not exactly known for the prowess with drones and have a much smaller inventory than, say, the Americans. Also, most of their Unmanned Aerial Vehicles are tiny compared with, say, a Predator."

"For example, the Predator costs about $21 million and would just about fit into a domestic garage. Most of the Russian drones were like big model aircraft by comparison."

"The one that crashed in Al Jubail was a medium-altitude Long endurance UAV – a Heron, actually. This is a much bigger device than those used typically used by the Russians and had a flight time of 40 hours. I'm not sure how the Russians came to have this one."

"The Heron is made by Israel Aerospace Industries and is usually used for surveillance. Confidentially, from what we can make out, the Heron crash was the result of an anti-UAV defence system made in the UK."

"The defence system is called Blighter and is used to set up an electronic wall that the drones can't penetrate. The defence looks a bit like a small tank and has a big gun type unit on the front used to send signals that jam the drone."

"This one was being used for some trials when it activated against the Heron and pulled it into Saudi airspace."

"What were we doing with one of these anti-UAV units in Saudi Arabia?" Tyler asked.

"Maybe a coincidence? It was actually there for a demonstration, at the Jubail Naval Airport. The fact it found a real device to practice on was considered a coincidence."

"When the drone crashed at the demonstration, we, the Brits, located its hard drive used for covert filming. Someone managed to clone the disc before it was all handed over to the Saudi Army.

"Now, here's the thing," said Marcus, "Photos on the drive with

Russian subtitling were all of oil installations around Saudi Arabia and other parts of the Middle East. The Heron was mapping detail of oil installations for use by the Russians."

"It makes sense," chipped in Tyler, "Fix the currency, fix the oil and know what the competition is up to."

"Are we drawing too many conclusions from a few scant facts?" asked Rosie.

"Yes, you could say that," agreed Marcus, "Although it is probably our best working theory."

The Building Theory

"I need a cigarette," said Rosie. She fumbled into her bag and then slipped out of the door of the office.

"I can't tell whether this is personal," said Marcus.

"What do you mean?" asked Tyler.

"Well, the threat seems to come to two of the main buildings involved in the report. They could not know who wrote it because the names are behind department functional designations."

But if you think about it, the report has travelled from here, St Martins-le-Grand, to Warwick Lane and then on to Hammersmith. After that, it would go to GCHQ, but I'm wondering if it has got that far?"

"I'm not sure I follow you?" questioned Tyler.

Marcus stood up and walked across to a whiteboard. He wrote down the three names of the buildings. Then Marcus drew arrows between them. Then he added GCHQ.

"I guess that they are trying to flush out the people involved with the report. That's us, Tyler, plus your friend Matt, and Rosie."

Tyler shook his head," Where would they get that idea? You've only just told me about the roubles and the oil?"

"I know, but whoever 'they' are, they probably think that you and Matt knew more than you did in practice.

They'll have identified Matt because of his direct manipulations of the market in his crypto dealings."

"It should be much harder to identify me," Tyler mused.

"The whole point of the way that Matt and I had set up the cyber coin thing was to preserve Matt's anonymity in the background," Tyler explained.

"Yes, but it didn't work. You both had access to the bank account, for example. That's how we found you both," continued Marcus.

Tyler looked concerned, "So do you think they are after us?" he asked.

"That would be my best guess," continued Marcus.

The door opened, and Rosie entered the room.

"It's always useful to go for a cigarette," she said. "Do you want the latest news?"

They nodded.

"There's been another bomb call. This one is targeting Hammersmith. I was with Geordie from Facilities. He said there would be a general alert issued to this building as well."

"Okay," said Marcus," It looks as if they are working along the document route."

"We'd better tell the other teams," said Tyler.

"I think we can tell them about the bomb alert, but I think we should keep our theories close at the moment," said Marcus.

"I'm not sure whether there is a leak, the bombs seem to be just a little too precise."

Tyler looked at Rosie, who nodded. "Yes, we'll keep it close. For now, at least," she replied.

Rosie was already getting ready to go outside the building to smoke another cigarette. The shock of the news had just tipped her over the edge.

"You don't want to be doing that," said Tyler, "You'll be chain-smoking by the end of this!" There was a muffled noise. A sharp crack followed by a low thud. The glass from the tall windows in the office rattled. Grey paint chippings dislodged and fluttered down.

"That was not Hammersmith," said Rosie. "It was much closer."

They could hear the alarm system start.

Part of the bomb protocol was to not go out through exits close to the site of the bomb. Training had also taught that a secondary detonation could create even more destruction.

"I think we may be better to stay in here," said Marcus. "We are in the core of the building a long way from the roadside."

They could hear the noises in the corridor people of hurrying towards exits. There were the shadows of men in full body armour walking past the office area.

Geordie appeared," They've already brought out the special services. They are to provide us with additional protection while we work on this."

Buzzback

The emergency services kept the team on lockdown for several hours.

When Tyler was eventually allowed to leave the office, he was surprised to see his phone buzzing away.

It was like getting off a plane, but he'd not switched the phone to silent or airplane mode or anything. Then he remembered that the police had a system which could render phone cells inoperative within an emergency zone. It was a way to stop remote triggering or remote comms between terrorists.

They must have switched cellular comms back on again.

He looked through the messages. Mostly it was people he knew who wanted to know he was okay. He decided to create a single text and send it to everyone.

Then he noticed a call from Erica. He was quite surprised because since they split, there'd been no real communication except for few practical matters, like what time the van would pick up the stuff.

Tyler decided to wait until he was home before calling Erica. She only lived a couple of miles away, but he hadn't seen her since they broke up. Then, the other side of a couple of beers, he called her. It would be the first time since she'd moved in with Drew. But she had said it was quite important.

The phone rang, and she picked up almost immediately.

"Erica?"

"Yes, Yes, I'm glad you called back. Thank you. Look there's something I need to talk to you about. Can we meet soon, please? It's kind of work-related."

"Er, yes, of course."

"This is YOUR work-related, Tyler. Look I know something about what you do and think this might be useful. I saw your building on the television tonight."

"Where shall we meet?"

"How about the pizza place? The one that does those salads?"

"Tomorrow, lunch, midday?"

"Sooner? Tonight? Maybe nine o clock? It is important."

"Erica? Are you sure? I can be there if you really want..."

"See you at nine."

Tyler heard the click. Erica had gone. An express train of a phone call. He recognised her professional financial services business voice, even if he didn't know exactly what it was that she did.

Tyler took a taxi to the pizza place. He wondered if she would be alone. It would be easier than with Drew as well.

It was a Monday evening at the Franco Manca, and there were several empty tables, even one in the far corner. The waitress that greeted Tyler recognised him and asked where he would like to sit.

Tyler gestured towards the table in the far corner, and she smiled and took him across.

"My friend will be joining me soon," he said, and then just as he was sitting down, Erica arrived. She spotted Tyler and came straight across.

"How about some wine?" Tyler asked. The waitress was still by the table.

"That's fine," she answered, "Some Pinot Gris, please."

"Me too," added Tyler.

The waitress nodded and hurried away, some sixth sense telling her that this was going to be a fast turn-around table.

"I think I said this was work-related?" Her eyes were looking directly at Tyler; he melted slightly as he remembered how gorgeous she could look.

"Yes," he answered, "I think you might have mentioned it when we were speaking earlier."

"But," she said, "it's delicate because it probably relates to the work you are doing right now,"

"I saw the news today and saw your office building was bombed, or, at least I think it was your office, it looked as if it was in any case."

"I know you were doing something financial and clandestine for the government, but you were always vague about what it was. The reason I'm speaking to you is that I think there's something odd happening at our bank at the moment."

Erica had never really talked about the bank other than her time there with Drew, so Tyler didn't even really know what she did.

"You know that I work in the trading area?" she asked. Tyler nodded as if he knew what she did.

"Well, there's been some strange developments in the last few weeks. First of all, Drew's boss suddenly disappeared. He worked the Russian desk and was in charge of the financial position that we run."

"It's all very macho in our bank, and the dealers are like predatory animals in the way that they operate. Imagine a casino full of people gambling with someone else's money," she added.

"I thought you liked working for the bank?" Tyler asked.

"Sure, it's quite prestigious to be there, but the reality is very cut-throat and misogynistic." she added, "For example, they just fired my friend who got pregnant."

"The whole place is a hire-fire culture - get up or get out," she added.

"I'm surviving there rather than thriving. I'll get another big bonus this year but, to be honest, after that I'm probably going to find a way to leave," she continued. "but look, this is about Drew's boss and what happened next," she continued.

"So, we've been dealing with Russian currency and also the Russian foreign exchange position over the last few months. Everyone knows that there's been some shakiness and that Russia has been managing the position based partly on oil reserve balances," she continued.

"Drew's boss - his name is Victor - had anyway been looking very stressed for the last few weeks. Now, all of a sudden, he has disappeared. It was actually about a week ago.

"Drew told me that Victor was putting on the screws. He was

asking us to bet against the market. As if he knew that Russian Central Bank would bail out the rouble at the last moment."

"What, like insider trading?" Tyler asked.

"Oh definitely," said Erica. "But I'm not saying this if you understand me. Not whistleblowing - not until I have next year's bonus, anyway."

"But I don't think Victor would be doing this off his own bat. He is a ruthless shit, but even he would draw the line at something so obvious that the PRA would pick it up very quickly."

The waitress returned. "Have you decided?" she asked.

"A salad for me," said Erica.

"Which kind?" asked the waitress.

"The one with butternut squash," said Erica.

Tyler remembered that he had been living on pizzas for the last two days.

"And me too, a salad, with chicken," he added.

"Any more drinks?" asked the waitress.

Tyler looked at Erica.

"We're fine," said Tyler, and Erica nodded.

"...So why are you telling me this?" asked Tyler.

"Your job," said Erica," It's something to do with analysis, isn't it? Like we have financial analysts to run the markets. The only analysts I can think that the government would have are either for Treasury or something sneaky."

"I'll put you into the sneaky department, after some of those things you did with Matt," said Erica.

For the first time since she'd appeared, Tyler saw Erica smile.

Tyler remembered that he'd told Erica more about his role than he was probably supposed to. He'd been newly into it and excited, and it did have that subtle air of mystery. Erica knew Matt too, and he was sure that she'd have heard more from him.

"Okay, I think you have got my job pegged, yes we are interested in what has been happening with Russia," he sighed.

"Right, here's the thing. Victor had lunch with Drew about a week ago. They went to Rules for a wine-fuelled blow-out. A right PFL. Victor seemed very agitated. Drew said he'd never seen Victor like it before. Well, it's fair to say that Victor is a bit of a bastard. He can swear his way out of many situations and has the classic reputation of a bully-boy banker. On this occasion, he said to Drew that a Russian named Pakashenko or something had been pushing him for the rouble layoff to be increased.

"We were in the process of doing it, although the whispers were of insider trades. Pakashenko or his bosses seemed to want our bank to make everything happen much faster. You can't, of course, because it'll trip Reporting and then we'll have the regulators down on us."

"Now for the delicate part. Drew isn't squeaky clean in all of this. He's been following the lead from Victor and selling derivatives based on the rouble through some pretty weird financial instruments.

"You know about Quantitive Easing? Where the Bank of England prints extra banknotes to help manage currencies? Well, we're seeing this happen now, except it is as if Russia is somehow making the money.

"That's why our bank is confident that the Russians can dodge their way out of trouble by using foreign exchange. They seem to have a mysterious excessive amount of FX at the moment.

The salads arrived. Erica picked at hers.

"So, we have a foreign government running quantitative easing in another currency?" asked Tyler.

"Yes," said Erica, "And it is under the radar at the moment. They are somehow generating foreign money to bail themselves out."

"And that's when Victor disappeared. He started to tell Drew about the situation he'd got himself into with Pakashenko, and then disappeared."

"But without Victor, there's no-one to drive the bank's position?" asked Tyler.

"Oh, there is all right, get dug in deep enough and it is like a self-playing piano," Erica smiled again.

"Victor had grown the position so that the regular trading algorithms would kick in and maintain it. To be honest, that's what Pakashenko was probably annoyed about. The bank will manage the positions conservatively when on auto-pilot."

Tyler pushed his plate away, "Is this just happening in your bank, do you think?"

"I doubt it. Victor has a little gang of friends spread out around the other big players. I'm guessing that at least some of them are in on the action."

So, what do you want me to do?" asked Tyler.

"I'm worried," said Erica. "A couple of the newswires were hinting at Russian involvement in the bombing. You and Matt know about cyber-money. Victor has disappeared after a heated exchange with a Russian and Drew is implicated in all of this. I thought if I told you, you might be able to think of something. I don't want to have an ex that's been blown up, nor a partner that's in jail."

"You know about Matt? Asked Tyler.

"Matt what?" asked Erica.

"I am sorry to have to tell you this, but Matt was reported as the single casualty from the first bomb," said Tyler.

"Shit..." said Erica, "It's started. Look. Thanks for the salad. I'm going back now. Call me if you can think of anything."

"Love ya," said Tyler.

"No, you don't," said Erica, smoothing her skirt as she prepared to leave the restaurant.

Kangaroo

Tyler read a short report from Rosie. The second explosion had been similar to the first, mainly upward, creating limited damage and no casualties.

Tyler turned up for work as usual but noticed Marcus and Rosie standing outside the building adjacent to a Mercedes minibus.

"Don't get too used to this," said Marcus, "but we're going for a short ride to another property."

Later that morning, they sat around their third new set of desks, sipping tea from mugs.

"I hadn't realised just how many additional buildings the Department owned, or at least inhabited," said Tyler.

"Yes, and the building looks quite normal from outside although inside this one there's a fair number of military," added Rosie.

"And I wonder if the disks will have exploded in the move?" mused Tyler.

"You've 'arrived' once you are in one of these buildings," said Marcus. "Now we've got top-level security. Greater, I'd say, than the overt security at Vauxhall Cross or in MI5."

"I guess that just means it could all kick off at any moment," said Tyler.

Rosie smiled, "So now we are proper secret agents!"

William House was one of those buildings that had been around for many years and also had running adaptations to keep it fit for purpose. These seemed to include much heavy wiring along the ceiling and blast protection for the doors. There were zoned layers of security, which Tyler found cumbersome to use, because of how frequently he needed his access card inside the building.

A one-time fairly plush looking staircase swept up to the higher floors and their office, which seemed like a faint replica of the one in Central London.

Tyler noticed that his floor didn't seem to have the armed security that was prevalent on the floor below.

"It's not like we are really in Hammersmith either," said Tyler. He'd noticed that the nearest tube stop was Earl's Court and the area close by was filled with small eateries and pubs.

"Welcome to Kangaroo Valley," said Rosie, citing the one-time nickname of the area.

"Not so much, nowadays," replied Marcus. "The Antipodeans have moved away. It is still a great area for undercover flat rentals, though. I had to stay here once, as part of an assignment."

"But we are off the grid, I take it?" asked Tyler.

"Oh yes, the story is we've moved to Hammersmith, and that's where our land-lines will point," answered Marcus.

Marcus added, "We've been moved here, Earls Court, as a

precaution. Two reasons. Firstly, in case anyone didn't like us. Secondly, as an additional level of security, in case of leaks."

"But they could follow us here?" quizzed Rosie.

"Not exactly," said Marcus. "It would presuppose they knew where we were staying."

"Wait a minute," said Tyler, "are we being held?"

"You are, and it is entirely within the terms of your agreement with the Department. We are all being held.

"The point of this is to ensure you melt away from public view for a week or two.

"I've had it happen to me before. It can be pretty reasonable. The Department will put you up in a hotel and supply you with new clothes and so on."

"So that's why we are in flat-land," replied Rosie, "Nice and cheap!"

Tyler thought about if this had happened earlier before he had broken up with Erica. It would have been difficult to explain. He wondered how he was going to explain what Erica had told him, to the others.

"I still can't quite see why they expect us to come up with something?" said Tyler, looking towards Marcus.

"It's because of that report I produced," he replied.

"They seem to think I had discovered something. But let's not kid ourselves, there will be several other teams like us doing this kind of thing as well."

"But what about all the people over in GCHQ?" Tyler asked. "Surely they will have more resource and better ability to find out what is happening?"

"That's the problem," Said Marcus.

"GCHQ and many of the American agencies are great at working out what has happened after it has happened. In other words, their ability to reconstruct events that have occurred is pretty good.

"It's not as smart when they are trying to predict the future, though. The two bombs are a classic example of this. They can probably try to work out how these bombs were put in place.

"Maybe they can work out who did it as well. But before the two alerts were given, we didn't have any inkling that this was going to happen.

"It is not a new situation, either. Each time something like this happens we are working after the fact. We've seen planes shot down with missiles. Planes exploding in mid-air with suitcase bombs. Random acts of carnage throughout the Middle East and other parts of Europe.

"And in each case, we are then expecting someone to investigate it and work out who did what. Take something like Lockerbie which happened many years ago. It took ages before anything was cleared up from that."

Marcus was shaking his head.

"The idea of using little groups like us is to try to find ways to predict and pre-empt things rather than to spend time in the archaeology of something that has already occurred," explained Marcus.

He continued. "Of course, I'm not saying that they don't ever discover anything through their information scanning methods. There's still plenty of smaller situations which are picked up. But it still seems to be the bigger situations and sometimes the random events like teenagers hacking into major banks, for example, that go unpredicted by anyone."

"Like Black Swan Events," said Tyler, "When something unexpected comes along, and everyone tries to rationalise it?"

"What was that movie with Tom Cruise?" Rosie asked. "You know the one where he has to go to stop crimes before they are committed? Total Recall?"

"No, Minority Report," said Marcus," Based upon that Philip K Dick story."

"I'm having you on my team for the pub quiz," said Rosie.

"Well, our situation isn't one where psychic mystics will pop up to help us solve it," said Marcus.

Erica

"The best things in life make you sweaty."
—*Edgar Allan Poe*

New Intelligence

The next morning, a bright Tuesday, Tyler planned to get into the office early.

To his surprise, both Rosie and Marcus were already at their desks. They were talking earnestly and looking towards a new wall chart which they had been building.

"We are building a timeline", said Marcus, "Trying to look for any gaps."

"The most obvious one to ask is when does the timeline start?" said Tyler.

"Good point. We have just been discussing that," said Rosie

"It covers the period from when I wrote the original report up to the second bomb," said Marcus.

"Here, let me take you through it," said Rosie.

"Back in February, we get the first trickle of curious currency transactions. It is what sparked Marcus to take a look."

"It's as if someone was testing the water to see if it all worked and would be undetected," added Marcus.

"Then Marcus writes his paper. Fact-based but probably inconclusive- No offence, Marcus -. The paper works its way through the system in March and April," said Rosie.

"It's also low profile, and there's so much else happening that it would probably slip through the net undetected," added Marcus, "I didn't even believe in it that strongly."

"Now that's when it would probably take a second paper to hit the system to provide some corroboration," said Rosie.

"But there's nothing, except a faint register of interest from the Genesis team."

"Who?" asked Tyler.

"That's the team where your buddy worked. Matt was on a team that looks at small situations which could amplify to have large repercussions."

"Yes, this seems to point to someone with prior knowledge of the manipulations. Someone who could drive the agenda, I wish I could have thought of that when I was writing the report," said Marcus.

"Yes, but you know so much more now than you did back in February. There's no wonder it was passed over," answered Rosie.

"I think I have something to add," said Tyler," About the currency manipulation."

He went on to describe what he had heard from Erica, although he was reluctant to name his source.

Both Rosie and Marcus seemed interested, but Rosie almost immediately asked the obvious question, "So how can you substantiate this? You are relaying this to us anonymously from a friend of a friend. It won't stand up and could get you into hot water."

Tyler looked at the floor. "Some of this is quite personal, so I'd respect your discretion. I got this from my ex-girlfriend, Erica, who works for an international bank, in the trading area. She told me all of this last night, but it was in confidence. She'd seen my office on TV, heard that there were whispers of Russian involvement and was worried for me as well as for her boss Victor. He's the one that has disappeared."

Marcus nodded. "We'll need to get a statement from Erica. I could pull another bar stunt if you like to get an area cleared where we can record what she is saying. It's not exactly police procedure but should be enough for our investigations."

"Marcus, just a reminder that Erica and Drew are well-heeled bankers. We'd better find somewhere appropriate. Not our local boozer."

"I'll have to ask Erica nicely, although she seemed genuinely worried yesterday," said Tyler.

Tyler called Erica once more. She accepted the invitation to come along to a second meeting but asked to bring Drew as well. Tyler considered how awkward this second session would be and tried to imagine how Marcus could attempt it in the local pub.

Steak

Marcus arranged a venue, which was close to the Bank's main building in Canary Wharf. The restaurant had some small private tables, and one of these was selected for the meeting with Erica.

Tyler and Rosie took the tube across London to Canary Wharf and then zig-zagged through the many walkways towards the restaurant. They arrived at 17:15, which was around 15 minutes before they had all agreed to meet.

Marcus was already in the restaurant.

Tyler looked at the set-up. It was fine white linen and fancy cutlery. The menu comprised Argentinian steak. Marcus has done well. This was Erica-level dining. Erica and Drew arrived at 1730 precisely and were shown in, greeted, seated, and everyone was poured an aperitif.

"Champagne cocktails, how lovely," said Rosie.

"Erm, watch out they contain tequila," whispered Tyler.

Tyler noticed that Erica asked for "just the Brut Royal, please," just the champagne, then.

Tyler began, "They've asked me to introduce everyone." He

described Erica and Drew as two of his acquaintances and Marcus and Rosie as two co-workers. He knew it was better to be bland and to allow people to manage their own disclosures.

Marcus then asked Erica to tell the story. The same one she had already told Tyler.

Erica almost immediately deferred to Drew, who gave an account of his recent meeting with Victor. Tyler asked Drew if he had heard any more of Victor since that day.

"No," said Drew, "and the Bank seems to be taking it rather well. None of us has heard any more, and last week his desk was being cleared. They told us a new manager is being brought in for temporary continuity."

Rosie asked, "What happens when someone is taken out of the team like that?"

"It happens quite often," said Drew and Erica nodded.

"The Bank is very performance-led, so when people don't make their targets, they are replaced quite quickly. There's a whole process for this."

"Yes," said Erica," The HR team were involved, and it looked like a routine if sudden, replacement."

"But wouldn't there be a memo or something? And email to explain the sudden departure of Victor?"

"Oh, there was," said Drew, "It explained that Victor had gone to another organisation, implied he had quit suddenly and that is why they would not provide any forwarding. It's not that unusual."

"I tried calling his mobile but got 'number unobtainable'. I even tried his home number but got the same. He lives somewhere around here, in an apartment in Canary Wharf, he's divorced although I think his family live somewhere in Essex. I've not tried to visit his home, but I do have the address," said Drew.

"Okay," That will be useful said Marcus," We can check up in case this is all a worry about nothing."

"I doubt if you will find him there," said Drew. "He is a noisy bugger, and I'd have expected that one of us from the team would have heard by now where he's gone. He'd also be trying to poach us by now."

"So you suspect cover-up?" asked Rosie.

"It depends, but if the Bank had worked out what he was doing, with the Russian trades, then I'd think we would be adjusting the position and trying to cover the tracks," said Drew.

"But there's nothing, no position adjustments and the AI-systems are maintaining the same holdings. It's surprising because no-one has come after me, checking my trades or anything."

You'd better give us his phone number and address, then," asked Marcus.

"We can trace back to see whether there is anything even more unusual."

"One moment," started Drew, "I think I'd better give you his other number, too. We have Bank issued phones, which the Bank can track, but most of us also carry a second personal phone. Anything irregular would appear on that."

Drew hunted into his pocket and produced a phone. Rosie noticed it looked like the one Drew had placed upon the table at the start of their conversation.

"Yes, I know. It does look the same. It makes it easier not to get spotted with an obvious burner phone," said Drew, noticing Rosie's quizzical look.

"So aside from what you've told us about the rouble trades and Victor's disappearance, is there anything else that you want to tell us?" asked Marcus, "Is anyone else behaving unusually? Are there any other systems that seem odd?"

"You've not worked in a trading environment?" said Drew. "There is nothing normal about the day-to-day. It's like a crazy-farm most of the time. But in honesty, I can't think of anything else."

"Me neither," said Erica.

"Look, "said Drew, "Victor was pressuring me on this, you know."

Marcus nodded, "To be honest, I'm more interested in the bigger picture than in some bonus-making scheme that you and Victor concocted. I'm sure it will serve you well at the end of the year, or whenever the bonus gets awarded. For now, I want us to carry on with our investigation."

Drew nodded, and Erica shuffled in her chair. She looked at her watch. Then Drew did the same.

"We need to be somewhere," said Drew, "Bank business…we fitted this in at the last minute."

Tyler knew the moves by Erica. She was extricating herself from an awkward situation.

"I'll see you out," he said.

They made their way towards the stairwell. On the way, Erica said, "Look, I've told you all we know. I hope you won't need to involve us any further. I did this because I was concerned about what was happening in the Bank, and partly because I thought you and Matt had been wrapped up in some Russian currency stuff in the past."

"I get the message," said Tyler, holding up his hands.

Erica stepped closer to Tyler.

"Look, don't do anything stupid. Here's a memory stick. It's got a useful selection of transactions on it, Drew pulled them from Victor's records yesterday. They are Private and Confidential."

Tyler nodded, "Thank you, thank you," he said.

"I'll ask Rosie and Marcus to keep both of you out of this. If there were any other way to have this meeting, then I'd have taken it."

Drew nodded, and they both stepped out onto the pavement. Tyler could see Drew already beckoning to a cab.

SanDisk Ultra Luxe®

Tyler was immediately nervous about the memory stick he had been given. What if it included any trace routines? He couldn't use it inside the office, because it might give away their location. It could also get Erica and Drew into trouble.

He decided to take it home and to put it onto his home laptop. He could still examine it, but it would de-risk any search routines. Then a thought occurred. He could get it copied onto another media for safety.

His route from Canary Wharf took him along a couple of rainy streets, mid-evening in London. There were mobile phone shops next to the kebab shops. He decided to drop into one. He recollected that some of these shops had to handle the most spectacularly tawdry of files and folders, so a copy of the memory stick should not present a problem.

"As-salaam alaykom," said the owner, as Tyler pushed past the door and the beaded curtain into the small shop. It was a mobile phone shop and money exchange and cafe. There were a couple of small tables out on the street.

"Wa Alykom As-salaam," said Tyler, remembering his manners. He'd been around these parts of London a long time and knew the basic greetings.

"Hello, do you want some internet time?" asked the man behind the counter, in good English.

"No, thanks, I'd like this little stick copied if you can do that?"

The man looked over to the memory stick and called out to someone from the back of the shop.

A young boy appeared; Tyler guessed he was around 12 years old.

"yumkinuk naskh hadhih aleasa lileamil?" asked the man behind the counter.

"Yes, I can copy the stick for the man in about ten minutes. You will need to sell him another USB stick, though."

"You hear that, fi hawalay 10 daqayiq, in about 10 minutes, you can have a copy. You'll need to buy another stick though."

"That's fine," said Tyler, "How much are the memory sticks?"

"kam nubie bitaqat aldhaakirat?"

"Ten pounds for 32GB - SanDisk - good make," came the reply.

"That's fine," said Tyler and looked in his wallet for a banknote.

"Thank you," he said, addressing both the man behind the counter and the young boy.

The boy took the stick away and a few minutes later returned.

"Here, it's done. Original and the copy," the boy produced the original memory stick and a bright green generic USB flash drive.

"A moment," the boy said, and he took the flash drive and plugged it into a nearby laptop.

Tyler could see the directory structure appear. The boy had, indeed, copied the stick.

Tyler reached again into his wallet.

He looked at the man.

"Here," he said as he handed the boy a banknote, "Thank you."

The man nodded, and the boy smiled.

"Mae alsalaama!" said Tyler,

"Goodbye", said the man.

Tyler pushed back through the plastic curtain into the night's rain.

Food shopping

Outside, Edgware Road bustled with its typical visitors. Some called the area Little Arabia, but Tyler knew it, as did many Londoners, as just one of many multicultural parts of London, showing off its cosmopolitan character.

As he exited from the shop, he noticed a couple of people who he'd seen earlier in the day. He suddenly wondered if he was being followed.

He surreptitiously moved the two memory sticks apart and then slipped one of them into an inside zippered pocket of his jacket.

As he did this, he paused outside of a shop window and looked inside. He was checking the reflection, and sure enough, he could see the two men he thought were following him appear to pause also.

He looked around and spotted a Marks and Spencer store nearby. The food shop would make a useful diversion to see whether they followed him inside.

They did, so he moved to the main aisles, picking a small basket.

He then slowly walked around the aisle, noticing one of the

men doing the same, although without bothering to pick up a basket.

He approached a security guard in the store.

"Look, I'm sorry to trouble you," he began quietly," I think that man is shoplifting. I saw him take something outside the shop just now and pass it to a couple of women."

The guard looked Tyler over. "Thank you, what did he take?"

"I'm not sure, but it looked like vacuum-packed food. Fish maybe, or steak?"

"Thank you," said the guard and then said something into his radio pack. Tyler heard an announcement come through on the shop's Tannoy system.

"Will Mr Liftly please come to the packing area?"

"Game on," thought Tyler as he slipped around to the store's alternate entrance, where he bumped into one of the people who had been following him.

"Sorry/Pardon me," they both said it at the same time. The other voice sounded American, softly spoken, possibly Canadian.

Perhaps it was just a coincidence?

Tyler slipped from the store. He was relieved to see that he was not followed.

Ten minutes later he was on a tube train, heading for home.

He put his hand in the pocket where he'd placed the memory stick.

It had gone. Quickly, Tyler felt for the other one. Still there.

The men had been following him. They had pickpocketed the memory stick.

He stayed on the train past his stop, then caught a taxi back to his home.

Discoveries

Next day, Wednesday, Tyler was early to the office, but once again, Rosie and Marcus were already there.

Tyler had dropped the memory stick off with some forensic analysts who could look through it for anything unusual.

The call came through.

"It comprises mainly business trades. Derivatives and Foreign Exchange transactions. Quite large amounts - hundreds of thousands to millions of dollars- which are then pushed through a Russian Bank, RKI Bank. Rossiyskiy Kiber Investitsionnyy Bank.

Russian Cyber Investment Bank?" guessed Tyler.

"Very good," said the analyst." That's where most of the transactions were cleared. There's another unusual repeating transaction though, it seems to be about 10% of the RKI cut, and it goes to Gun Street Holdings.

"Gun Street?" queried Tyler.

"Yes, that's right. We typed it into Google and got an old YouTube western movie and a song track. There's no corporate site or anything."

Tyler was alert now. Gun Street was a rather typical Matt-inspired name. After a Tom Waits song.

He was about to tell Rosie and Marcus, but Rosie started up a summary of their status.

"We haven't found anything new," said Rosie walking to a whiteboard, "Let's summarise."

She grabbed a marker pen, hesitantly tested it on the board and then wrote:

- Van bombs gave a warning;
- Drivers escaped via taxi;
- Explosive was PETF;
- Low yield explosions
- Victor Boyd disappeared
- Boyd's phone missing
- Possible Russian connection
- Cybercash?

Rosie wrote down three big Subheadings BOMBS, VICTOR BOYD and RUSSIAN MONEY.

"Well," said Rosie," The disappearance of Victor seems genuine. We have a summary from Nasreen's team. There is no passport record of him leaving the country, and there's no spending pattern from his credit cards. His wife thinks he is on a management course."

"How so?" asked Tyler.

"The management course phoned him at his ex-wife's home number. He is divorced, you know. They told his ex-wife, Chantel, that there had been a change of plan and that the course would now run for two weeks."

His ex seemed to think it sounded genuine.

"What about his phone? can you work anything out from the GPS?"

"That is slightly odd. Boyd's work phone was sending a signal from his current apartment. So far, the phone hasn't been located. Victor Boyd is living in a fancy apartment near Canary Wharf. We entered it, but there is no sign of anything untoward."

Tyler scanned through the report. The report was very factual, but the response from the Chantel did not look as if she was surprised that he has suddenly disappeared. It ran along the lines that he would do his own thing and was quite likely to be off somewhere else. She was not surprised if he had been involved in some kind of financial swindling either.

"Wow", said Tyler, "It looks as if there is no love lost there between Victor and Chantel.

"That's what we thought," said Rosie

Rosie added, "There's a couple of pictures of the house as well, it's out in the sticks on the borders with London. Chigwell actually, one of those footballers-wives' type houses. You know the kind of thing, gates, Range Rovers and a Porsche and a big semi-circular drive."

Marcus commented, "Yes, although the police report says that the house has been a family home for the last eight years."

"It also says that his salary and bonuses would be quite capable of paying for this kind of lifestyle. I don't think any rake-off money has been used to finance his day to day lifestyle - there's no need."

Rosie looked at the photos, "I wouldn't mind living somewhere like that." She paused, "or maybe it's a bit too blingy for me. Notice the Lions heads positioned either side of the electronic entry gates?"

"I think the heated pool would make up for it," replied Tyler.

At that moment, Nasreen entered the office.

"Hiya," she said, "How's it going? I thought it better to liaise face-to-face.

"We are still following that downed drone. We've loaded that information onto the server now. It's mainly oil installations in Saudi, but there are a few urban complexes on camera too. The drone seems to be using a mix of Israeli software and a Russian command and control language."

"Our investigation has taken a slight twist," said Marcus.

"There does seem to be a proper Russian connection, and it appears to be linked to rouble manipulation, similar to the report I produced a couple of months ago.

"We've just been talking to a banker about a possible infraction at his bank. It still doesn't tie together with the bombing of our offices, although it does seem to lead back to Russia.

"Yes, Russia is coming through loud and clear," said Nasreen.

"Either that or we are getting a massive misdirection?" mused Marcus.

"We are also chasing down the forensics from the bombs," said Nasreen, "So far it looks like mining explosives. Common and difficult to trace. Battery triggered PETN, by all accounts. That's penthrite, which has various brand names in the mining world. According to our specialists, a pure PETN releases little that can be picked up by detectors, so the manufacturers use taggants with it. That's special substances added to the mix which can be detected."

"I think PETN has been the go-to choice of aeroplane bombers too," said Marcus.

"I recollect the shoe-bomber used it and that it has been smuggled into ink toner cartridges too."

"I've just googled it as well." Said Rosie," One of the common brands for it is SEMTEX. One hundred grams of it can destroy a car."

Nasreen nodded, "You have a good team here," she said, looking to Marcus. "Let's keep one another briefed." Marcus nodded agreement, just as Nasreen's phone started to buzz.

Nasreen answered it, "Huh?" she said, "It doesn't make sense. Guys, the taggants are from a US batch of Semtex. Department of Defense - Air Force - It doesn't add up."

Nasreen put her phone down. It buzzed again, "Gotta go," she said, closing the door behind her.

Tyler had one further source of enquiry. He decided to call his ex-flatmate, Kyle. Nowadays, Kyle specialised in security and cybercrime.

"Hey, Kyle,"

"Hey Tyler, long time! How are you doing?"

"Doing good, well, er -actually- it's all a bit weird here."

"I'd expect no less; I've gone freelance, you know? I'm helping a big corporate fix their firewalls. It's amazing how much bad stuff comes in and out. Trousers down and all that. Speaking of trousers down, how's Erica?"

"Kyle - we split up, Yeah, Look I was wondering if I could pick your brains?"

"Sorry to hear it, man. Look, what do you need?"

"It'll be better face to face."

"Okay, tonight, are you still living near the old flat? I can get over to The Drayton by about seven if that's any good?"

"Brilliant."

The Drayton Arms

Tyler arrived at The Drayton Arms shortly before seven. He surveyed the scene of many fabled drinking bouts across the years when the three amigos would go out on the lash. Meekly, he ordered a Pride and sat at a table near the frosted window.

"Hey man," greeted Kyle, "Are we in for a session? Look what they've done; There's a theatre upstairs now!"

Tyler smiled, "Kyle, I need to pick your brains."

"You and Matt dug a hole bigger than you can climb out of?" asked Kyle.

"Not exactly," said Tyler, "But it is related to that cyber money stuff we were doing back in the flat."

Tyler described the situation to Kyle, who sipped quietly at his beer.

"Wow. That's pretty epic," said Kyle, "I knew e-currency would end in tears."

"But let's break it down a bit. You guys had stumbled on to a cyber coin mining process. But you could only mine at about 2 or 3 coins per week."

"Yes, that's about right," said Tyler, "and it was Matt that discovered the process, with that little computer rig he had in his bedroom."

"I remember," said Kyle. "The one I wouldn't touch with a bargepole."

Tyler smiled as he sipped at his beer.

"So, Matt must have been editing the blockchains that these processes use to create the currency?" said Kyle.

"He often talked about maintaining the blockchain integrity," answered Tyler.

"Yes, that's how this works. It is like a self-regulating process which uses hash keys to keep track of the individual coins."

Kyle paused," I think Matt must have found a way to edit an occasional extra coin into the sequence."

"One coin at a time, it could take forever to make any significant money. Okay, it's fine for a couple of students, but really? To make serious dosh, you'd need huge computing power. Not only that. You'd need a way to camouflage the operation so that it wasn't picked up in general auditing."

"You know what I think?" said Tyler.

"I think Matt had found a way to build new currency strands, and he was gradually populating them."

"I see, parallel to the main strands, like a cloned image. That would make the most sense," said Kyle. "And it wouldn't show up as much if it looked like a whole new number series. Like a self-contained sequence of blockchains. A parallel universe."

"Yes, that's what I wondered. Something fairly robust that looks as if it has integrity. So, what if I wanted to use this at a national level?" Asked Tyler. "Like to make millions of dollars?"

Kyle sniggered. "Millions? - Well, you could try it! You would need huge computers, though. Think about it. Making two or three coins a week from Matt's computers? This is no student project. It's immense."

"So, what if we have a nation-state behind it?"

"What, like the US, or China or Russia? That's what it would take, but I can't imagine it would be kept secret for very long," answered Kyle.

"And if it were a corrupt state then you'd have people taking money from the piles created," he added.

"Do you think this is what might be happening?" asked Kyle.

"I don't know, said Tyler, "and I don't know how we'd ever go about finding out."

"Two ways I can think of," said Kyle, "First of all, information leakage from the systems. Someone blabbing about something to do with it.

"Secondly, you could attempt to follow back along the blockchain links to see where the chain originated."

"How would I do that?" asked Tyler.

"Good question," said Kyle.

"Did you say you were working for the government? I presume they can afford my daily rates?"

"So, you are in?" Asked Tyler.

"Well, this one seems like it's legitimate," answered Kyle, smiling, "Unlike the old Matt hokey scheme.

"This time I'll be finding out just how tricksy it was to track down what you and Matt had been up to.

Kyle

"Prime numbers are what is left when you have taken all the patterns away. I think prime numbers are like life.

They are very logical but you could never work out the rules, even if you spent all your time thinking about them."

— *Mark Haddon, The Curious Incident of the Dog in the Night-Time*

Confer

Tyler made his way back across London to the office. Kyle had given him some new thoughts to share with Marcus and Rosie, and he still needed to tell them about Gun Street Holdings.

Marcus had already arranged a conference call across the river with SI6.

Tyler knew he would not usually be in on such a call, but he assumed that on this occasion, he already knew as much as anyone and so he would be called in.

Usually, he would enjoy the physical trip across the river to Vauxhall Cross, the well-known building housing much of the secret services.

Despite the makeshift nature of their current accommodation, Tyler was impressed to be whisked upstairs into a secure communication suite.

It was obviously where some of the top people worked, and he was amused to see little drinks stations and canapés in the entrance area.

Then he was ushered into one of the studios, where Rosie, Marcus and himself sat in a row, facing some large monitors.

The conference table was one half of an elliptical design, and the several flat-screen monitors placed to represent where people would sit.

Suddenly several people appeared on the monitor screens. The men wore suits, and the two women were both power-dressed. Tyler wondered whether they were from HR. Maybe they were all about to get fired? The whole setup was very corporate. On the monitors, they looked about life-size, and Tyler could hear little clicks and breathing sounds from the high-quality audio. If Tyler stretched out across the table, he felt as if he could touch them, although he noticed that two of them were in London and the other two in Cheltenham.

Marcus introduced the team and netted the story down. Tyler was quite impressed at Marcus, summarising such a complex chain of events into such a simple account.

Then Marcus added: "It's hard to see how this links to the explosions, but it is as if we have discovered something, written about it and then someone found out and is trying to flush us out. It isn't a protest or a warning; I'm pretty sure that someone is out to get us."

"So how does this fit with the facts?" asked one of the suited men on the call. He looked more operational, slightly scruffy with rolled-up sleeves and his tie at an angle.

"We can't fill in all of the gaps," answered Rosie, "But it looks as if the chance of discovery is something that they are annoyed about."

One of the suited men was typing something into a laptop. Tyler realised that he was communicating with the people present in the Cheltenham office.

"We don't have any hard proof about this," said the operational person. "We need to find someone directly involved."

Marcus nodded, "We think we may have such a person, but there's no way to corroborate what has been happening. The main person linking this together has disappeared."

Tyler wondered whether he should mention his conversation with Kyle. He decided not to say anything at this stage. Kyle could be a useful asset, but he didn't want him to be put off too early by the suits from SI6.

Tyler tried to work out who was in charge. It seemed impossible. He realised, suddenly, that no-one had a clue what had been happening.

"That meeting wasn't all that useful," said Marcus, as they left the room to go back to their own office.

"It felt more like an upload than anything, and even then, they didn't want our opinions colouring the situation.

They arrived, and almost immediately, Janice walked in. "Our team have found the first bomb van on the CCTV," she said. "We have managed to track it back to its origin and to follow the bombers."

She held up a photograph of the first incident along with what appeared to be some trace back photographs.

"The Americans call the use of vehicle bomb a form of poor man's cruise missile. We have a perfect example here."

She showed the van and then a couple of photographs of it in other parts of London.

"We've pretty good coverage, once we knew what we were looking for," she said. "And the vehicles were both parked for several minutes on double yellow lines right outside their targets."

"But we have to ask ourselves as well as what we got - the explosions - what didn't we get? Casualties - except for that single analyst who was outside of the first building. You'd expect the van drivers to have been caught up in it. But somehow the drivers managed to slip away. Look closely at these freeze frames. "

She held up the photograph from a traffic CCTV in the street.

"Can you see? It's indistinct, but there are some feet underneath or behind the van. Someone has climbed out and is getting ready to make off."

"But look, they don't reappear. Instead, we see a taxi has paused by the far side of the van. The van driver has climbed into the taxi."

"That wasn't a regular taxi. No, it was a planned pickup." Janice looked around the office for their reactions.

"Well, it certainly looks organised. Did we manage to get any other footage of the taxi?" asked Rosie.

"Yes, This later shot. We tracked the taxi for around ten minutes. It covered some ground pretty fast for Central London. Then you can see the passenger. He is wearing a hoodie and what looks like a tracksuit," answered Janice.

"It's a perfect disguise. Bland and anonymous. Also, the kind of clothing that could be shed easily, to change appearance," mused Rosie.

"Precisely," said Janice, "The taxi takes them to a store and drops them off. They go inside, and we pick them up again from the store cameras."

"Them?" said Tyler, "you mean there's more than one of them?"

"Two of them, they appear to be wearing scarves as well as hoodies," said Rosie. "Even those trainers look generic."

"The hoodies are baggy as well," said Marcus," But I think the taller one is a female?"

"Well spotted," said Janice, "Despite the low quality of some of the capture, we also thought that the movements of one were of an athletic man and the other of a woman."

"Do you think they wanted to be spotted?' asked Marcus, "I mean, they seem to have planned everything else?"

"I doubt it," said Janice, "We had to sift through acres of video to find these images. And you can rest assured that we've cross-checked it to make sure we don't have the wrong pictures pulled up."

"However, they were still using tradecraft to try to elude detection," continued Janice.

"They've gone to the clothes department, changed from their hoodies and reappeared looking respectable in casual clothing."

Janice continued, "They go to a back-exit from the store where they appear to pick up bicycles. You'd think with the number of cameras in use we'd still follow them easily enough."

"But of course, the cameras are trained to track number plates, so we don't know where the bikes have gone."

"That seems to be the end of the trail, although we do have some good quality pictures of them both in the store, after they had changed into their escape clothes."

Janice showed the final photographs. A tall, slender Mediterranean looking woman. A shorter bearded sub-Saharan African man, dark-haired and sturdy build, like he'd done weight training.

"IC2 woman and IC3 man," said Janice, "Game on."

Schmoonitary

Tyler had been looking through a massive database of possibly identifiable people. He had the two photographs of Persons of Interest that Janice had provided and was trying to match them.

It was soul-destroying work. The computer would riffle through dozens to hundreds of images and then present a screenful of around 20 pictures to be individually scrutinised.

"Scrub genius, insert detection", he said," Detection is 99% perspiration and 1% inspiration."

He wondered whether his blood sugar was low because every so often he found himself glazing over while watching the screens. It was mind-numbingly dull to attempt this with so many incoming pictures to compare with just a couple of real targets.

Tyler knew that Kyle's security world contact meant that Kyle had access to Artificial Intelligence scanning software. He decided to pick Kyle's brains once more about the situation.

"Hey, Kyle! It's Tyler again!" he announced as Kyle picked up his mobile.

"Hiya Tyler," answered Kyle," I'm in Tel Aviv at the moment, at a security conference."

"Oh, I hope I'm not interrupting a meeting or anything?"

"Nope, it's fine. There's a lot of sneaky stuff in the pipeline. It should keep you guys busy for years! I've just been to a session on battlefield smart-dust."

"I'd expect no less," answered Tyler, "Look, I'd like to pick your brains again. This time it's about image recognition AI software."

"Chinese are best at that," said Kyle, "Although coincidentally, quite a lot of the work has been done here in Israel. Or that's what the local developers would have you believe.

"What is it you want to do? Basic facial recognition, I presume? Looking for a needle in a haystack?'

"Yes, that's right," answered Tyler. "I've got the high-res originals and am trying to find out who they are."

"Well, the Chinese through firms like Megvii, Sensetime, Cloudwalk and Yitu have made facial recognition commonplace in China. They tag all the faces, add attributes and then cross-index. If someone is found, they progressively get their background data augmented and also the number of hits that they receive."

"I knew you would have some suggestions to help me." Replied Tyler.

"It's not that simple," answered Kyle. "The database that you'll need and the compute power to process the imaging are both pretty awesome. China gets away with it because, well, it's a totalitarian state.

"You mean it's a unitary one-party socialist republic?" said Tyler.

"Unitary Schmoonitary, we all know it's a communist dictatorship," said Kyle.

"So, if I mention these bits of software to my friends in Cheltenham, there' a good chance they will know what I'm talking about?" asked Tyler.

"Oh yes, they will know," said Kyle," Although our other friendly cousins, the Americans, are highly nervous about using any of this stuff. Imagine letting Beijing-authored software into GCHQ or the Pentagon. It's Huawei times a thousand."

Kyle added, "You know if you could find something on the Approved Products Buyer's list, you'd have more of a chance. The only thing is, the Chinese have a deployment track record. They use this stuff all the time when they are managing street protests and tracking down agitators. I'm not saying it is on the right side, but it is advanced."

Tyler grimaced. He realised that he could get help from British approved products, but they would not be nearly as powerful as software already being used in China.

"You know," said Kyle," There might be another way..."

Kyle continued," There's a couple of things you could try. First, you'd need to find out if anyone in GCHQ has access to any of the Chinese AI search engines. I think I can confidently predict that the answer to this is 'No'. Even if they have access, they are not able to exploit it. They'll have it in a testing lab somewhere without any external links.

"It negates the purpose of the software, which trawls around the internet looking for connections," continued Kyle," Trust me, our security firm would know if this was being deployed. The other related point is that it would need a decent server farm to operate. Maybe a thousand servers for starters. Get my drift?"

Tyler considered. He'd ask Marcus also, in case there were yet more things he didn't know.

"Then," said Kyle," There's what we do...This isn't a plug for my company, you understand, because I'm trying to be helpful here. We'd look around for leverage."

"Leverage?" queried Tyler, "What kind?"

"Not financial, systemic," replied Kyle, "I'd ask a question like 'where can we get access to huge server farms, advanced algorithms and parameterised search?'"

"Go on," said Tyler, "I can only think of Google and similar."

"Precisely," said Kyle. There's reverse search in Google, "Image to picture identification, but it is massively dumbed down so that when you ask for pictures of daisies, it will present flowers."

"I know about that," said Tyler," I - ahem - used it when I split with Erica to cross-check what she'd been doing."

"Too much information," said Kyle. "Although in practice you'd probably find that the information you got was 'styled'?"

"Er, yes, it did seem to find leather jackets and handbags similar to the ones that Erica was wearing."

"Yes, that's because the search you use is tuned to a commercial setting. It's part of the Google business model. You may have been looking for Erica, but it would start to give you styled advertising after the first few search items had been returned. Now imagine if, instead of seeking handbags and sunglasses, it could look properly for faces."

"I can see this working, but also that it needs a couple of things."

"Yes, a different search method, that's where a Chinese-style AI would be useful and - here's the even more difficult part - access to a decent photo library of faces. "

"I think we might just have that in-house," answered Tyler.

"You do, it's just that you are not allowed to use it."

"Passport photos, driving licence, Border Controls, they all provide exactly the type of photo to be searched, hook up an AI facial recognition and some galumphing great servers, and you'll locate those people easily."

"Can I take this idea?" asked Tyler.

Kyle smiled as he answered," JASMOP - Just A Small Matter of Programming - It'll cost you copious beer the next time we meet. And hints that I could be useful in some kind of upcoming project."

"Gotcha," replied Tyler, "Expect to hear from me again soon!"

Go, Chiefs!

Thursday, and Tyler was in the office early again. Rosie and Marcus were already there. He'd think they were having some clandestine affair if he didn't already know that Rosie's partner Vanessa often met her from their old office after work.

He also thought that Marcus had never mentioned acquaintances either male or female ever since he had worked there. A very private man.

"Good morning!" Tyler smiled as he placed his bag onto the scruffy desk next to all of the high technology equipment. "I've had an idea about tracing those two from the van. Marcus, you'll know how much of this is possible..."

He went on to describe the process of marrying reverse searches with an AI system and a new database of faces. He described it as "like the Chinese system," and mentioned the various software that Kyle had described.

Rosie nodded," That's a good idea, using AI. You know something, I can call up James Harding at counterintelligence operations and find out what we can do."

Rosie and Tyler assumed the pose ready for a conference call. This was not going to be as elaborate as the board room meeting. It would be a series of faces displayed on their computer screens.

The system made a noise that Tyler likened to a burping goldfish and then suddenly a face appeared on the screens.

"Hey James, how are you doing? How are The Chiefs getting along?" Rosie smiled at the screen.

"Rosie, you're looking fabulous, good to see you, and who are these other fresh faces you've been playing with?"

"James - meet Marcus - My Boss - and Tyler - they are both fully cleared so that we can have a very straightforward conversation about my current challenge."

"Ah yes, something to do with all the pops and bangs around London?" asked James.

"That's right; we are trying to figure out who did it," said Rosie.

"Mr Plum with the lead pipe?" ventured James.

"That's what we wanted to talk to you about; less lead pipe and more chopsticks," said Marcus.

"Interesting. So, what do you think you need?"

Rosie said, "Chopsticks is a clue. Do you have access, by any chance, to Chinese AI Image recognition software?"

"Maybe..." said James cautiously, "...Precisely who is asking?"

"I need to run some deep AI recognition like the kind that China is using in the protest marches, for crowd identification."

"I could possibly assist with that," said James, "Does it have to be Chinese?"

"What do you mean?"

"Well, I have a lovely line in freshly baked British and American software that does the same kind of thing. And a way to run it.

"We've been using GCHQ in collaboration with the NSA to build our database. Amusingly, the general public is our greatest asset."

Marcus nodded," So it is true then? All that Deepface stuff?"

"Yes, and more, the selfies that people produce are most helpful towards building the database and even li'l ol' Facebook's AI-based facial recognition software is remarkably accurate."

Tyler questioned James, "But isn't this illegal?"

"It certainly is, up to State level. Beyond that, well, it becomes pretty essential as the building blocks for national security."

Tyler interrupted, "I take it all of this is Confidential?"

"Tyler, this is more than Confidential, this is TOP SECRET - we don't want anyone knowing that we have such capabilities. Imagine the stink and noise from the Daily Mail and Channel 4."

Tyler nodded. He realised this was unwittingly unleashing vast state power.

Rosie continued, "Great, now we don't need to put this into an email, but I'm about to send you a couple of decent resolution images of faces. It would be a great test of the capabilities of your system to see whether they can be identified."

"Okay - are they British? We have a more limited capability to trace non-nationals. Unless they have come into the country, of course. You'd better send the source files as well; in case we can pull anything extra from the binary.

"We seem to have a meeting of minds here," said Marcus. "And we'll owe you a team box at Sandy Park."

"Lovely to see you, you rascal, Rosie," said James, "Cheers."

"Cheers," echoed the others as the line went dead.

"What was that about Sandy Park boxes?" asked Tyler.

"James sounds quite keen on the Rugby. I guessed a VIP box at the Exeter Chiefs would be his idea of heaven," replied Marcus.

Dolly the Sheep

Friday morning, Tyler was awoken from sleep by the phone. It was Kyle.

"Hey man, I've been thinking. You know the thing about data centres? It could be that we've been thinking about this all wrong. Instead of it being something big that's being used to crunch the data, perhaps it's being done another way. Remember, in the old days when we used to use ordinary PCs for gaming? And we moved to the bigger and more dedicated devices so that we had enough power?

"Well, nowadays there's a massive amount of computing power available in the distributed Internet. I don't mean the Internet that everyone uses from their smartphones. I'm thinking about all the smaller permanently attached devices.

"For this to work at scale, there would need to be a well-distributed network of powerful computers to provide the mining. They would also need to appear to come from different geographies too, so that they did not trip any alerts when they were clearing such sums of money."

Tyler could see where Kyle was heading with this but let him continue. Armies of bots churning out cybercash. He didn't think it would work.

Kyle continued, "It got me thinking. Bot mining is like another universe waiting to be exploited. Then I thought of what other alternative universes could there be? It came to me. Just make the blockchains 'stand-alone' instead of part of what is already out there.

"So, I went through a couple of those transactions that you sent me from the memory stick and traced them back to the original blockchains.

"They were as difficult as any other to penetrate, but I could see that they had started from some different seed values. It's quite clever because they could still appear to be regular currency, but the base from which they are created is different."

"Like plausible fakes?" asked Tyler.

"Yes," said Kyle, "If this money were in use with other transactions, then it would soon be detected as different. Because there is such an extensive network of worldwide friendly repositories, then the money is in effect held in a separate condition where everything looks right.

"I guess we'd call it part of the dark matter used within the world of finance.

"The smart part is using a bank like the one you have been talking to, as a way to be able to turn these transactions back into some other form. In effect to launder the cyber coin back into some other currency.

"Ultimately, the bank is processing fake cyber coins, but it doesn't realise it, because the entire blockchain that has been created looks plausible.

"Doesn't realise it or is turning a blind eye?" asked Tyler.

"Could be but it's amazing how dumb the markets are. Aside from a few propeller heads, it's full of barrow-boy salespeople and their friends. Remember, when people shorted the money markets with sub-prime mortgages packaged up to look respectable? It's a similar idea. Dress the blockchain up to look presentable, and plenty of people will trade it, especially at an advantageous rate. Hey, Dolly the sheep looked real enough."

"I suppose the secret is not to make it look too good to be true`?" asked Tyler.

"Exactly," said Kyle, "That would be a giveaway. It makes complex derivatives a brilliant suggestion because, to be honest, hardly anyone understands how they work. It's like putting a recognisable envelope around this kind of misty transaction.

Kyle was getting quite excited now, "There's no reason they couldn't be quite a few versions of this in use at the same time.

"The only thing that would blow it is if too much cybercash appeared and all of a sudden, the whole financial network was swamped with surprising amounts of suspicious liquidity.

"Whoever is running this has been quite clever because they have limited the flow to just the amount needed to stabilise the Russian currency.

I asked Kyle, "So can you prove any of this?"

"I've only got those sample transactions at the moment," he said. "The ones on that stick you got from your girlfriend."

"My ex," corrected Tyler," Erica is my ex-girlfriend."

Kyle coughed, "Well, look, if I had more transactions and some help then perhaps I could dig further into this and we may be able to track down how it's generated. And where it goes after it has been generated."

"Okay," said Tyler. "I think your days as a consultant for the government are just about to start. You'd better sharpen your estimating pencil."

"Even better would be to penetrate the bank system and get our own snooper device plugged in?" suggested Kyle.

"Yes, just like in Mission Impossible. I'll order the suction cups and wires."

Tyler noticed the note of enthusiasm in Kyle's voice. He thought about the difficult conversations ahead.

Hotel

Friday, and Tyler was surprised. For yet another day, Rosie and Marcus had been in the office when he arrived. And he had been progressively starting earlier each day.

"Rosie?" He asked," How on earth are you getting in so early? I thought you had the longest commute."

"That's right, I do. But I thought Marcus told you? Now we're on this special assignment we are staying in the hotel across the road. It's a lot more convenient with these long hours. And we get some level of security included too."

Tyler immediately thought of soft linen and minibars.

"I've been schlepping my way back to my flat and all the time you are staying a couple of minutes away. And it looks like quite a nice hotel too?"

"Oh, it is," answered Rosie, smiling.

Marcus had reappeared and been listening. "Sorry, Tyler, but it's for people who are grade 7 and above," said Marcus. "Rosie and I both qualify, but I'm afraid you're still too junior."

Tyler groaned. "What, even if I am the potential target?" he muttered.

Tyler noticed that Marcus and Rosie were both holding a similar sheet of paper.

"You jest," said Marcus, 'But we're the ones who are being threatened."

"Why, what's happened?" Tyler said, looking worried.

"Yes," said Rosie, "Fresh threats through the post."

"But I thought we were already threatened?" Tyler said. "...Surely those threats were pretty much as bad as it can get?"

"Take a look at this," said Rosie, waving the paper towards Tyler.

Tyler took the paper, which looked like a letter to Rosie from the hotel management. One of those letters that gets pushed under the door when it's nearly time to check out.

Instead, this was a message addressed to Rosie, which said, "Leave it alone." It was signed by the hotel manager.

Tyler looked worried.

Rosie explained that both she and Marcus had received one of the notes but had thought it was some bad taste practical joke from one of the other teams staying in the same hotel.

Evidently, this was a warning to show they knew who Marcus and Rosie were. And that they didn't like the work conducted by the Department.

"So," Tyler asked." Are we about to move to yet another location?" He wondered if this would give a chance to get a hotel room for him as well.

"So far I've asked security to look into this for us. At the moment we are upping the security for the hotel. It's something done routinely with that hotel in any case."

"We now have our floor and the ones adjacent secured as well as some of our people guarding the whole location," said Marcus. "Even our hotel access keys have been re-coded ."

"It's like the security we have here?" Tyler asked.

"That's right," said Rosie, "Except our guys in the hotel are not wearing uniforms…Yet."

Colder War

Afternoon and the TV news in the office showed pictures from Turkey. Marcus looked up at Matt and Rosie.

"You'll have seen it in the news; there's quite some activity between Turkey and its near neighbours. These are possible examples of The Colder War in play.

"I've picked up on some possible Turkish moves that could be made by Russia."

"This is since the elections, and the USA decided to get all huffy with Turkey?" asked Rosie.

"Yes. The Russian courtship of Turkey has already involved the Russians moving away from the construction of the South Stream natural gas pipeline from Russia across the Black Sea to Bulgaria.

"When Putin cancelled the South Stream project, he replaced it with a natural gas pipeline that goes across the Black Sea to Turkey from the Russian Federation's South Federal District. It makes a desirable option for Turkey."

"Turk Stream with Russian energy giant Gazprom can link with Turkey's Botas. Moreover, Gazprom will start giving Turkey discounts in the purchase of Russian natural gas that will increase with the intensification of Russo-Turkish cooperation."

"That would give Russia oil and gas access to the EU and supply balancing via the Turks?" queried Tyler. "It's quite clever and low risk for Russia as long as Turkey is allowed to remain stable.

"Of course, they would need a tame banker to broker such a significant situation. They would need someone who can be a free agent but is well-linked to major banking players. It could be incredibly lucrative for such a player.

"Yes," said Rosie, "and that might be a lead?"

"Ordinarily I'd agree," said Marcus, "but the sheer amount of money that Russia can now generate means it has stumbled across a way to keep Turkey on-side, based upon an ongoing series of well-placed payments."

"Bribes?" asked Tyler.

"Exactly," said Marcus, "Although they are 'easy to generate' bribes in the sense that Russia can order the money from the cyber fraud."

Rosie added, "So this deal between Ankara and Moscow creates a win-win situation for both the Turkish and Russian sides?"

Marcus continued, "Not only will Ankara get a discount on energy supplies, but Turk Stream gives the Turkish government what it has wanted for years. The Turk Stream pipeline will make Turkey an important energy corridor and transit point, complete with transit revenues. It's like a legitimate Silk Road.

"Legitimate only in the sense that the Russian currency input can't be detected," said Rosie.

"In this case, Turkey becomes the corridor between energy supplier Russia and the European Union and non-EU energy customers in south-eastern Europe. It's brilliant," said Tyler.

"That will surely piss off the Americans, particularly as it becomes a near-neighbour supplier to the middle-east? Come to think of it; Turkey can also position itself as part of the middle east when it wants to."

"Yes," said Marcus, "Turkey can be Middle Eastern, European or Russian tinged, as it sees fit. Not a bad puppet for Russia to be able to manipulate."

Rosie nodded, "So then Ankara gains some new leverage over the European Union and has an extra negotiating card with the EU too because the EU will have to deal with it as an energy broker."

Marcus continued, "Yes, so accidentally, the US Colder War policies are creating a whole new set of advantageous plays for Russia."

"It only works because of the cyber currency," said Tyler, "Without that, the whole situation could look very different."

"I agree," said Marcus, "but right now, Russia has been on a spending spree to de-risk its pipeline building. Moscow could have wasted resources and time building the South Stream to see the project sanctioned or obstructed in the Balkans by Washington and Brussels."

"If the European Union wants Russian natural gas, then the Turk Stream pipeline can be expanded from Turkey to Greece, and also to other European countries that want integration into the energy project. It positions Russia as an interesting player in the region."

"Interesting," said Tyler, "I can think of a few other words!"

"The cancellation of South Stream also means that there will be one less energy corridor from Russia to the European Union for some time.

"This boosts chances of a settlement in Ukraine, which is an important transit route for Russian natural gas to the European Union. Inevitably the European Union will want to push the authorities in Kyiv to end the conflict in East Ukraine."

"Turk Stream and the strengthening of Russo-Turkish ties may even help placate the gory conflict in Syria," said Marcus, looking grim-faced.

"If Iranian natural gas is integrated into the mainstream of Turk Stream through another energy corridor entering Anatolia from Iranian territory, then Turkish interests would be even more tightly aligned with both Moscow and Tehran."

"This is what Russia wants and sticks it to the USA," said Tyler.

"Yes, and someone gets very rich on the skimmings," said Rosie. "I'm sure this could be a lead."

Marcus nodded," A characteristic of a liberated totalitarian country is the rise in illicit payments and the sudden increase in wealth of a few well-placed individuals with access to power. There's a lot of ex-State civil servants who are nowadays oligarchs."

Marcus continued, "Turkey has already been on a tightrope over some aspects of the Syrian conflict. Ankara has had to craft an understanding with both Russia and Iran not to let politics and their differences over the Syrian crisis get in the way of their economic ties and business relationships.

"At the same time, Washington has tried to disrupt Irano-Turkish and Russo-Turkish trade and energy ties like it has disrupted trade ties between Russia and the EU."

"What, diplomatically?" asked Tyler.

"Not just diplomatically," there was also the assassination of the Turkish Trade Minister in Paris a few weeks ago. That threw a massive spanner in the works," answered Marcus, "I even wondered if America was trying to heat that particular discord."

"So, the Russian State appears to be making a grab for oil rights and at the same time using fake money to prop up the rouble. And it is using cyber cheats to achieve it?" asked Tyler.

"That's what it looks like," answered Marcus.

Evaluation

I want to stand as close to the edge as I can without going over.

Out on the edge you see all the kinds of things you can't see from the centre.

— *Kurt Vonnegut*

Blockchains

They were in the Raglan.

It was a pub close to their original office. Rosie was to meet a slightly peeved Vanessa to tell her that she would be away for a while longer. She'd asked Tyler to come along to verify the situation to Vanessa and to try to keep it light-hearted.

They'd been waiting half an hour, and Tyler was buying the second round. He sat down at the well-used brown table. "Cider and a pint of Doom Bar," he said.

"So come on," said Rosie," Tell me about blockchains. I know the general theory that they are used in making e-cash, but you'll have to explain it."

Tyler smiled as he remembered his own lack of knowledge when he started working with Matt, from around the time that Matt brought the first little computer into the flat.

"The blockchain is an ingenious invention. A way to safeguard large amounts of cyber-money," answered Tyler.

"Blockchain was devised for digital currency and micro-payments, but nowadays, the technical community has found other potential uses."

"And this is relevant to the Russians how?" asked Rosie.

"I'll come to that. Think of the blockchain as an incorruptible digital ledger of economic transactions that can be programmed to record not just financial transactions but virtually anything of value."

Rosie clinked their glasses together. Tyler sipped his drink.

"In the simplest of terms, the blockchain is a time-stamped series of records of data that are managed by clusters of computers not owned by any single entity."

"No one owns it?" asked Rosie, "What about the Russians, then?"

"Just a minute, let me finish. Now each of these blocks of data (i.e. block) are secured and bound to each other using cryptographic principles (i.e. chain)."

"I see," said Rosie, the blocks are linked together by chains, using secret codes?"

"Kinda, yes," said Tyler, "But the 'secret' is public.

"Unlike a bank, with its central governance, these blockchain networks have no central authority.

"Now the part about the Russians. Unlike the secrecy of a bank's hidden ledgers, this is a very open system. It is a shared and immutable ledger; the information in it is open for anyone and everyone to see."

"Ahah," said Rosie, "One of those examples where its strength becomes its weakness?"

"Exactly," smiled Tyler, "Anything built on the blockchain is by its very nature transparent, and everyone involved is accountable for their actions. It plays directly to an unscrupulous state actor advantage."

"You see, falsifying a single record would mean forging the entire chain in millions of instances. That has been considered virtually impossible.

"Not if you are a government?" questioned Rosie.

"Yes, perhaps, or a vast company spanning many locations," answered Tyler.

"You see, the blockchain infrastructure carries with it a cost, but the transaction cost is, essentially free. That's how the information is passed from A to B in a fully automated and safe manner.

"It's who bears the infrastructure cost that becomes an interesting question, and how they hold everything secure."

"I see," said Rosie, "There's an angle on this."

"Yes," nodded Tyler, "Especially as the system moved away from micropayments."

"It was one thing to handle five-dollar micropayments for listening to a pop album or reading a book, but by the law of unintended consequences, very soon these payments aggregate.

"I see - Vast piles of $5 bills under the bed?" asked Rosie.

"Precisely," said Tyler, and not only that, the e-cash created became a tradable currency too. Through speculation, the $5 bills became worth $10 and more very quickly."

"Take Bitcoin. They started with a strike value of $13.50. They're worth over $10,000 now and peaked in 2017 at around $19,000. They are more than $5 bills under the bed now. They've turned into gold bars."

"So, no prizes for guessing that others would soon be taking a look?" asked Rosie.

"That's how I first got involved. We were speculating on the ability to create a new cyber coin and then to cash it in," said Tyler. "We wanted to make them and then turn them into real money.

"Here's how it works: one party to a transaction initiates the process by creating a block. This block is verified by thousands, perhaps millions of computers distributed around the net.

"See, that's where the big infrastructure is required. And the verification can be regarded as a 'black box' too. Ideal for someone unscrupulous.

"But let's see what would usually happen. The verified block comes out of the 'black box' and gets added to a chain. That chain is stored across the net, creating not just a unique record, but a unique record with a unique history."

"Hmm, Vanessa must have been delayed," said Rosie, looking at her watch, "Hey and thanks for coming along, you'll know when to leave, okay?"

"Sure Rosie, it's the least I could do, and let's face it, drinks with two lovely ladies, what's not to like? Let's see, where was I?" Tyler continued,

"Cybercash collapses the market-maker models that some of the high tech startups have enjoyed. Music, books, and so on can include micro keys that are flipped and will release payments to the music maker or the author. Such a technology would disrupt even Amazon and Alibaba. The micropayments go straight to the originator. That's why Facebook joined the party."

"But even if the original idea started that way, there are more basic forces at play."

"Take the financial world: The uses become more apparent.

Blockchains can change the way stock exchanges work, the way that loans get bundled, and the way that insurances are contracted.

"All of this legitimises the cybercash. Instead of it being something that only gamblers and nerds use, it suddenly has an economic value.

"Instead of gatekeepers, bankers will become advisers. Stockbrokers will no longer be able to earn commissions, and the buy / sell spread will disappear."

"Yes, but what has this to do with the current Russian situation?" asked Rosie.

"Well, think of the blockchain sequence as a pile of money. Quite a large pile in each sequence generated. Imagine if this fell into the hands of organised crime. Imagine if it fell into the hands of organised state crime..."

There was a scraping of chairs. Vanessa arrived and briefly hugged Rosie.

"Woman of mystery, what's happening now?" she asked, and she turned to Tyler, smiled and said, "Hello, and you must be Tyler! Lovely to meet you!"

"Let me get your drink," said Tyler as he rose and gestured towards the bar. "G and T, please," said Vanessa, "ice and a slice of lime."

"Coming up!"

Tyler made his way to the bar. He could see that Rosie was trying to explain her absence to Vanessa. He decided that he'd show the travel arrangements inconvenienced him even more as a way to show Vanessa that everyone was in the same boat.

Tracking

Janice tapped on the door of their office and walked in. She looked to Tyler like a TV presenter, perfectly groomed and always on top of her game. He noticed the way she smiled towards him but could then zone him out while she was talking to Marcus and Rosie.

"Hi Marcus, we've been following the drivers of the second van."

"We know they may be proxy drivers, of course, put up to the job without realising what they were doing.

"We need a lucky break on this somewhere now," said Rosie.

Janice nodded, "Yes, both of the trails to the individual bombings go cold although the style in each case is similar. They drive the vans to the outside of the building.

Tyler remembered, talking to Janice once, that she was a details person. She'd told him a story about something that had happened the previous day when Janice had visited an aunt in Southwark. The story was banal enough, but Tyler remembered that Janice held the detail and described the minutia with such a passion that he could see how she'd got the job in C-SOC.

"They park the vans, conveniently in one case on double yellows. and in the other case in a restricted area.

"The drivers slip out of the cabs and are picked up by a taxi almost immediately. It looks as if the driver of the taxi was part of the escape process. There also seems to be another woman passenger in the cab both times.

"What about smartphone footage?" asked Rosie.

"Nothing useable, you'd expect there would be some, but it's all from after the explosions and filmed from quite a safe distance. Amazing really that there are so many smartphones taking selfies but then when something dramatic happens it melts down to a couple of shaky hand-helds.

"You'd think with all the fixed cameras in London that we'd be able to pick them up easily enough. We've got footage of the aftermath of both bombs, but nothing aside from traffic cameras that track the time before.

"Then, when they jump into taxis, it goes cold. There's not much interest from anyone in filming taxi passengers.

"What about in-cab footage?" asked Rosie

"No, both times the taxi was running on false plates. They were clones of other taxis, designed to get through the ANPR without tripping any alerts. They used a couple of cab identities from Upminster which would be parked outside of the camera zones."

"We think they have ditched the cab somewhere and changed appearance again. It smacks of a slightly too easy trail at this point."

"What, like they wanted to be followed?" asked Tyler.

"No, more the idea that if we tracked them, then they would give us something tangible to track," said Janice.

Janice continued," However, the good news is that we traced the woman accomplice. She was present on both occasions with the drivers as they were ferried away by taxi.

"I assume the taxi had false plates?" asked Rosie.

"Yes, it did," replied Janice, "Although we could trace the false number plates in any case. Guess where the second car went?"

"An embassy, maybe?" asked Marcus.

"Marcus, the genius! Yes," said Janet, "Although not what you might expect. It went to the Chinese embassy."

"Can I take a look at the photographs we have of the suspect?" asked Marcus. "Are there any hints that he or she could be Chinese?"

Janice shook her head, "No. There was nothing that gives any real information about the actual suspect, Just the ability that we have to track movements. It corroborates with the first cab when we identified the IC2 woman.

"Look, here's the video footage of the suspect car on its way to the embassy."

She flicked video footage onto the screen behind Tyler's head. He moved around to see it more easily. First, there was a car moving away from a car park. It looked like the parking lot inside Battersea Park, close to the Zen temple.

"Not even an underground car park?" asked Tyler.

"No, I suppose the advantage of the Battersea one was the speed of swap-over and multiple park exits. It does assume that there was only one getaway car also," said Janice.

The footage flipped through a few cameras. Across Chelsea Bridge, towards Sloane Square, then Sloane Street, past some other embassies, into Pall Mall, towards Marble Arch and then a turn inwards to the east and toward the Chinese Embassy, after a couple of small zig-zags. It was a fairly direct route, the sort that an experienced London driver would take to avoid some of the traffic hot spots, while still being direct.

The car appeared to go into another car park close to the Chinese embassy.

"It looks pretty clear cut," said Janice. "They've taken the suspect to a place of diplomatic immunity."

"Which bomb is this?" asked Rosie, "Is it the second one? We had a route via a hotel flagged up for the first one. This route seems different?"

Marcus was looking at the route. "It's a good route, and there's hardly any traffic hold-ups," he said.

"Except around Belgravia. Look at the section by the outside of The Lanesborough Hotel."

Janice rewound the video, and they could see a brief hold-up in the traffic moving towards the busy Hyde park corner junction. Despite the driver's best efforts, there had been a short delay at that point.

"Look," said Rosie. "It's just like the other one. While they stop, someone gets out of the car on the kerbside. They are going into the back entrance of the hotel."

They looked at the footage. It was from a TfL camera on the roadside of the car. Tyler could make out the movement that Rosie spotted. The passenger and another person had left the car and moved across to the hotel in moments.

Janice looked, "We missed it," she said. "Damn, we've all been following the car to the endpoint, expecting one destination and then being surprised by the other. So, is he or she stashed away in the hotel, I wonder?"

"I doubt it," said Rosie, "I think the two of them will move on as quickly as possible- like in the first sequence. We'll need to get some footage from the hotel now to try to work out what has happened."

"The Lanesborough also has an entrance around the other side, onto Knightsbridge," said Marcus. "It would make an obvious way to switch to another vehicle and then plan a different route."

Janice nodded. "We are already following up with the Chinese Embassy, although you can imagine the diplomatic complications involved. We don't want to be accusing them of planting bombs in London."

"It's a great diversion," said Marcus, "getting us to follow a wrong trail, particularly when it creates such a lot of diplomatic ripples."

Janice nodded. "Of course, we will need to continue with that line of enquiry. If nothing else, we don't want them to realise that we may have discovered something. Meantime we'd better now examine the Lanesborough for any footage."

Marcus nodded his agreement. "I think we also need to check the rest of the route back again, he said. If they've pulled this stunt here, they may have done it at some other point. I noticed that the driver's route went directly past about half a dozen other embassies.

"I agree," said Rosie, "although I think the most noticeable stop of the car was outside the Lanesborough. Also, the embassy squares like around Belgravia are completely plastered with cameras so it would be harder to pull the same stunt."

"Marcus is right though; we need to look out for any other signs of an exit from the car. Mostly the car was moving, and the route is generally well exposed for good camera coverage. The Lanesborough is a clever spot because of the almost continuous traffic jams along that part of the route."

Tyler knew it would take another couple of hours to get the video footage from the hotel. Someone would be dispatched to get it and bring back as much as possible to be analysed.

"We'll need to see the exit from the hotel now and then need to follow to another location."

They all knew how difficult this would get if the suspect had left via another exit and then melted into the crowd.

Driscoll's Interview

"Three-Two-One."

"Good Morning continues now with a Live Interview with Gerald Driscoll, Minister for Internal Affairs.

"Thank you, Mr Driscoll, for joining us live on this politics section of Good Morning.

Driscoll sat, suited and wearing a blue tie. He thought himself the very model of a prominent minister and would not be caught off guard by these media types.

Driscoll replied, "Good Morning."

"Mr Driscoll, you have said you are not happy with current security measures deployed in the protection of the United Kingdom. That is like admitting you carry responsibility for the roles, while also indicating a need for fundamental change.

"I'm pleased to report, as I'm sure you know, that no-one was killed in what amounts to two terrorist bombings at central London locations."

"Mr Driscoll, we've seen two bombings, both seemingly with vans used to deliver the payload, at different locations within a couple of miles of one another and both within Central

London.

"Do you have some comments on the current situation?"

"Well, first of all, let me say at a personal level that my heart reaches out to each and every one of the people affected by these two terrible attacks on the fabric of London. We are working now with the Met Police, City of London police, military and other security services to both identify the perpetrators of these outrages and also to instigate further steps to secure ourselves against further attacks, or indeed any worsening of the situation."

"Well, Mr Driscoll, you were heard to say at your recent party conference that the current security service was too fragmented and that you would be instituting some reforms. Is it now a case of too little or too late?"

"What I said at the conference was part of the broader debate about changes to the ways that we need to operate the Ministry for Internal Affairs and the related security. It is part of the healthy party debate that we will always run to define the next stage of our government's direction on important matters."

"But you said that the security service was too fragmented. Isn't this another sign of that? There was no prior warning, nor do we know with any certainty who has placed these two bombs in Central London."

"The broader debate is continuing. The recent disruption to our two offices emphasises the need for further action," Driscoll realised he had let a cat from the bag.

"Your offices? Are you saying that the bombs were at your own offices? The reports say that the offices were smaller central London buildings?"

"I'm not able to comment on the specifics of the buildings concerned. It is not appropriate to examine this line of discussion.

"But Mr Driscoll, you appear to be saying that the attacks were not, as previously thought in the press, at some general and non-specific locations, but indeed were at your own buildings in Central London."

"As I have already said, I cannot comment on the specifics nor the occupants of the buildings in question."

"We already know that the security services have a major headquarters on either side of the River Thames, including famously the building at Vauxhall Cross. You appear to now be indicating that in addition to the two buildings, plus the entirety of the GCHQ operation in Cheltenham, that you also have further offices throughout London. Is this a symptom of the fragmentation you have referred to in your recent speeches?"

Driscoll's beads of sweat were being picked up under the studio lights.

"I cannot comment on the specifics of the security services and their use of properties within London and beyond. Suffice to say that we are examining all options for future reorganisation."

"Isn't it a bit late to be making these kinds of statements? We've just seen two big explosions in one of the major capitals of the world, yet so far, no trace of who is responsible. What concrete steps are you taking to capture the perpetrators?"

"We are examining the evidence from the two bombs. They both used a small amount of high explosive, and in both cases, the vehicle used was driven to the outside of the target and then detonated remotely.

"I think most of your viewers will have seen the outcome from the numerous television and other media reports."

"What else can you add to the information about what has

happened, and the steps taken to investigate? For instance, do we consider this terror-related?"

"I'm sure you will understand that a matter such as this is very sensitive. I cannot divulge information during a sensitive stage of an ongoing investigation."

"Mr Driscoll, so what exactly can you divulge at this stage?"

"I can state that we will take swift action to neutralise terrorists rather than to simply deploy cordons around incidents. I have already instructed for the deployment of special forces to take necessary actions against any future situations."

"Mr Driscoll, the question remains how you will know where to take these swift actions? It does not look as if your advanced monitoring is providing any advanced warning of events?"

"We are stepping up the monitoring of suspected terrorist activities. We will be stringently enforcing the ring of steel around the City, for example."

"This all sounds very well, but isn't it a case of closing the stable door after the horse has bolted?"

"We have a wide range of countermeasures at our disposal. I am not able to discuss operational matters with you at this time. Let me remind you that the UK has thwarted seven major plots so far this year, although most of them are also too sensitive to be exposed to general media."

"Mr Driscoll, with everything you are saying shrouded in such mystery I'm not sure that we quite know what to believe. You seem to be telling us that there have been seven plots this year including the latest which appears to be attacking your own clandestine operations. Is this providing a good role model for security services?"

"As I've said, we are taking active measures to manage and prevent any further expansion of the current terrorist activities.

I cannot say more because of operational sensitivities."

"Will that include heightened proactivity on the streets? Mr Driscoll? Will this include further escalation – for example the use of armed force on London streets?"

"I'm always committed to operating within the existing law, that means that any armed action by the police has to be proportionate to the threat. That is always the test put when it comes to any incident when police apprehend anyone."

"Mr Driscoll, surely that stops short of proactively stopping anyone in the act of a terrorist atrocity? It sounds as if you are not prepared to go as far as a shoot-to-kill policy?"

"I'm not happy with a shoot-to-kill policy in general – I think that is quite dangerous and can often be counterproductive. We need security that prevents people from firing off weapons, where they can. There are various degrees of doing things as we know, but the idea you end up with a war on the streets is not a good thing. Surely you have to work to try to prevent these things happening, that has to be the priority. We cannot reap a whirlwind from ill-judged actions."

Marcus and Rosie had been watching the interview.

Rosie winced at the last remarks.

"So, what is he allowed to discuss? It looks as if he is dancing to avoid answering any questions," continued Rosie.

"Yes, that's right," said Marcus. "There'll be a soundbite with 'whirlwind' and 'ill-judged' in it. I think his approach gives our department a bad name."

I sometimes think that's what he wants," added Rosie, '...and shoot to kill from the police.' He didn't have to rise to that bait."

"Wait until the news slot," said Rosie, " I doubt whether any of us will come out if it well."

Amanda Miller

Amanda Miller had been called for a meeting with Bernard Driscoll. She had seen his fairly lame interview featured on the evening news. "Shoot-to-kill, reap the whirlwind, ill-judged..." So much for media training.

She hated the annoyance of him calling her across the river from SI6 to meet him in Westminster Place. He was an arrogant bully usually, and this was the kind of thing he would do in the middle of a critical operation to show his importance.

Amanda had taken one of the company cars with a driver to get to Westminster Place. It had taken her across Vauxhall Bridge and then along the north bank of the Embankment towards Westminster Place.

It was one of those buildings that had secret tunnels underneath that lead in various directions. It included a tunnel across the road to Parliament and another route that went all the way to Downing Street.

Amanda assumed that Bernard Driscoll would be in an imposing room with his back to a big screen probably with a couple of flags and other paraphernalia to emphasise his importance.

Driscoll was an inept man but made up for it with puffery.

Amanda Miller knew her way around most of the corridors within Westminster and had previously needed to use them on several occasions as part of high alert situations.

This time it was different. Although Amanda had been called across, it was not clear what the purpose of the specific meeting would be.

Driscoll wanted a private meeting and not with his usual entourage of hangers-on involved.

Amanda approached one of the entrance areas to the meetings complex tunnel system.

"Ms. Miller," said the receptionist. "Are you ready?"

The receptionist smiled towards Amanda although still went through the formality of requesting her pass card.

"Look to the camera, ooh, I like that scarf," she added as she handed the photo pass back and an additional lanyard badge with her photo, a green stripe and GD-V3 printed on it in a large typeface.

Amanda was not affronted by this standard protocol when there was a heightened situation. She dropped the lanyard over her neck and stuffed the scarf into her bag.

She had already been through the metal detectors and glass turnstiles on the way into the building.

"I'll see if Mr Driscoll is ready for you," said the receptionist.

Amanda knew that the receptionist did not mean anything by this, but she still felt that Driscoll would probably take some time on purpose just to show his self-importance when they were due to meet.

Amanda had worked in other countries where there was

sometimes a kind of protocol that you would need to wait longer for more important people; It was their way of showing their self-importance. She knew better than to try to protest about this and prepared herself for a long wait.

Amanda knew the clock was ticking on the alert, but there was little she could do until after the meeting with Bernard Driscoll.

To her surprise, Bernard Driscoll came out of the door behind the receptionist.

"Our Miss Miller," he said, "Thank you for coming along here to meet me."

"There is something I would like to discuss with you that is very sensitive."

"I think we may want to take a short walk outside while I discuss this with you," he said.

Amanda Miller knew that the area that covered the reception and probably most of the meeting rooms incorporated full closed-circuit television and microphone monitoring.

"It's quite cold outside," she said, "But we could go for a walk along Parliament Street."

She reached back into her bag for the scarf.

Amanda knew that Parliament Street was also well stocked with video cameras. Still, there would be no sound recording except directly outside of Downing Street and the adjacent buildings on the west side of the street.

"I thought it would be better to take a walk towards Westminster Bridge," said Driscoll. "I can then also get some more cigarettes."

"They made their way from the building and into the busy street."

Amanda's car and driver waited in the underground car park close to Parliament.

She could call it back within a couple of minutes but still had to go through this theatre with Driscoll first.

"Oh," said Amanda, "Why the private meeting?"

"It's a disaster," said Driscoll, "this whole bomb thing is a disaster. I have the entire Ministry for internal security, the offices at SI six, MI5, GCHQ, and the special departments we set up, yet we don't seem to be able to prevent bomb attempts in central London."

"This is on you, Amanda," he continued.

"The Prime Minister called me in today and said this needed to be brought to a swift conclusion."

Amanda could sense that the shit was already travelling downhill.

The Prime Minister will have given Bernard Driscoll a grilling about all of this. Now it was his turn to start to look for a scapegoat. She knew what he would be saying next, well approximately what he would be saying next.

"I take it that everyone is already working on this?" Driscoll asked.

"Yet we don't seem to be any closer to even identifying who has delivered the bombs that have blown up outside two of our security offices?" he said.

"As London goes about its business today, it is more reminiscent of the old days when there were Irish terrorists planting bombs around London.

"This is bad for everyone."

Amanda decided to let him continue to vent. She was sure he would be coming to some point sooner or later.

"Fortunately for us, no members of the public have been killed in these attacks so far.

"Although the very act of setting off explosives in the high-profile parts of central London is bad for all kinds of reasons.

"We get bad press coverage everywhere, and we also look ineffective against this kind of attack.

Amanda mused, "No, this is on you," but she held the thought.

"We also have a huge budget for internal security, including the various agencies I've already mentioned.

"I'm going to need someone to serve up over this." he said," I think it will need to be those new departments we created.

"I need you to work on two things now," he said.

Amanda thought to herself, "he is about to get to the point."

She could see he was almost quivering with a sort of internal rage. It must be very uncomfortable to be Bernard Driscoll. A puffed-up politician with no real idea of what is going on. Only the ability to huff and puff as a way to try to resolve anything.

She mused at the incongruity of the two of them walking along the street together. She was, tall, svelte and toned, next to a round blob of a man, with just too much power. The Peter Principle personified.

"Of course," said Amanda, "I will see what I can do to expedite this investigation. You are welcome to come along to our control centre to see this properly," she said.

She knew she was slightly bluffing with this because although they did have the major incident room, so far that was little to show apart from the locations of the two bombs and the incoming claims against the bombs from very dubious sources.

It was uncharacteristic. Usually, there was a flurry of people wishing to claim a connection to bombing attacks even when they had nothing to do with them.

"Look," said Amanda, "I know you didn't bring me over here to give you a standard debriefing. And the fact we are now walking along towards the River Thames tells me that you want this to be quiet."

She didn't add her thought," and you want to do this in a way that you can threaten me without being on camera."

"That's right," said the Driscoll," They need this tied up, suspects identified and apprehended as well as internal people identified for removal."

Amanda looked towards Driscoll; he was trying to make sure that he dodged all of the blame. She also knew that he would have no reservations about landing her in the problem if he couldn't find anyone else.

"It's simple really," he said, "After you've sorted out the suspects, I want you to find a group to close down. I can't directly tell you to close the new departments, but I think this is the area which is of least use to us."

"The whole point about those small departments was that they were able to act autonomously away from the big processes that we run in the mainstream unit," said Amanda, "They are the equivalent in security terms of start-up organisations."

"That may be so," said Driscoll," but we need a much firmer command and control system operating. I can't have these little units running loose and still not delivering for us.

"Okay," he said, "Here is my shop to get some cigarettes. I think

I can take it from here."

Amanda realised that the meeting with Driscoll was over. He was as bad as ever; all he wanted was that someone else was to take the blame for the bombs and the lack of intelligence ahead of their detonation. He needed a scapegoat, and he also wanted to bluster his way towards a resolution of the situation.

Driscoll provided no real help, suggestions, or anything practical, just the typical bullying expected from him.

"Goodbye, then," said Amanda as she turned back towards Parliament. Driscoll continued into the shop, oblivious. Amanda reached into her pocket to her phone which she'd picked up on the way out from the office. The recording was still running.

She pressed a button on the phone and called through to her driver. As she walked back to Parliament Square, her driver parked outside the Houses of Parliament next to a couple of police officers. One of them opened the door for her as she climbed into the car.

False

"Back to the office?" Asked the driver.

Amanda considered. "No, I think we'll go to Earls Court instead."

Amanda decided that it would be prudent to visit Jim and his team at their relocated department offices. She had known Jim for many years. They had both been through a range of operational duties, and their paths had crossed many times.

Jim reminded Amanda of what a secret agent would look like if he were eventually retired from active service. Fit, alert and intelligent, he had been given the C-SOC Department to run when he transferred from Vienna, where he had run the small field station.

Jim had worked in other operational zones including the Paris and the Berlin offices. Amanda had been further afield mainly into South America. They had both seen their share of active service during their time although Amanda's was a more apparent high-profile situation based upon the type of characters in the various South American countries where she had operated.

It was primarily a matter of fate that Jim had been moved into the start-up of a new Department while Amanda benefitted from affirmative action to rise through the ranks inside SI6 and was now several grades his senior.

Jim and Amanda got on well and could usually read one another.

On this occasion, she thought that she could visit Jim ostensibly to offer some comradely support while they were going through the difficulties of trying to track down the bombers.

She smiled inwardly as she remembered Jim's old nickname, that of Jimbo. It was better than the one he'd had when they worked together in Berlin.

Of course, there she had another agenda as well, which involved the rather unsavoury request from Bernard Driscoll.

If ever anyone needed a nickname, it was Driscoll.

Amanda decided it would be easiest to explain Driscoll's blame game directly to Jim.

"Do you want me to call ahead?" Asked the driver.

"No, that won't be necessary." Said Amanda. She would enter unannounced, and it would add a certain frisson to the situation at the Department.

Sometimes a little theatre was a good thing.

She knew this would make no difference to Jim, who was equally wise to such manoeuvres, but it would make a difference to some of the staff to see her arrive and go directly to Jim's office.

Once inside the building, Amanda was taken directly to Jim. She wore her recently issued Parliament lanyard as she walked through the outer office, but then removed it before she went in to see Jim.

She could see several of the other staff looking up as she arrived.

She knew there would be some speculation about the reason for her visit.

She had already prepared a simple cover story for Jim regarding this, to offer the full support from SI6 for anything the Department required.

"Amanda!" smiled Jim.

"I am slightly surprised you are here in person, but it is always good to see you," he beamed.

"You are no doubt here because of some problem?" he asked.

"And it's not that difficult to guess what this is all about."

"That's right," said Amanda. "Two bombs exploding in central London within a few hours of one another, both of them at our buildings! You can guess that the Minister is pretty upset!?"

"No surprise there," said Jim, "and I expect he is already looking for a scapegoat. It's not me, is it?"

"I'm afraid so," said Amanda, "it's being targeted towards your Department this time. He wants to close it."

Jim scowled and then shook his head.

"He is so predictable. Has he offered any practical suggestions?" asked Jim,

"Nothing at all. And we are also drawing a blank over at SI6. I've also tried within GCHQ, but they don't have anything, despite vast funding. We can see that a couple of vans were used to deliver the bombs and that the bombs themselves were small. However, they were high-quality material. Military-grade, actually."

"And the credible threats from externals?" asked Jim, "Everything I've seen looks like it's opportunistic rather than anyone that knows what has happened?"

"That's right," said Amanda," We have not been able to track down any useful suspects so far."

"And we are still also trying to figure out the correct motivation for all of this."

"The message from Bernard Driscoll is that there will need to be a public sacrifice at the end of this," said Amanda. "Jim - He is asking for your department at the moment."

"I thought I'd pay you the courtesy of coming over here in person to let you know what has been said."

"Driscoll must have been beaten up by the PM over this. He was clearly rattled and did his usual puffery. That meant taking me outside to the street and then under the pretext of him buying some cigarettes he told me to find a way to shut you down."

"This is all about his control over everything. He hates it that we've been set up semi-autonomously" said Jim.

Amanda nodded, "Yes, that's right," she said," I sometimes wonder whether he is that interested in the humdrum matter of national security?"

"No, I think his main motivation is self-preservation and finding ways to continue to climb the greasy pole," said Jim.

"Though is there anything I can do to assist you at the moment?" asked Amanda.

"I know our units are already exchanging information on a routine basis about all of this."

Jim nodded. "There's nothing really that we can do until we find something tangible to use as a lead," he said.

"The nearest we have found so far is a pickup for one of the drivers which appeared to head off towards the Chinese embassy."

Amanda nodded, "It looks to us as if it is a false trail laid deliberately."

Jim said, "Someone is trying to point a finger towards the Chinese for this, although I am not convinced that this has their approach about it."

Amanda nodded.

"Yes," she said," Your people have provided some of that intelligence across to us."

"I think you managed to trace back the taxi that seems to be used as part of the escape route and then somehow link that to a getaway car.

"Yes," said Jim," And of course we have a cloned vehicle, and all the usual tradecraft that we see more often from our Russian colleagues."

Jim Cavendish

Jim Cavendish had become used to dealing with tricky situations in his small department. He knew Driscoll was unfair to target him and not because of failure from his team. They worked well together but were always a source of a kind of departmental jealousy which meant that other groups tried to shift the blame or lack of budget towards C-SOC.

Ever since the agreement to set up the new unit as if it were a start-up enterprise, he had to deal with the more conventional parts of the Service. The parts that wanted him to shut down,

Fortunately, the track record from the team had proved influential with several situations creating a positive reaction.

Jim still realised they were still on a knife-edge, and the recent situation with the bombings could quickly overshadow the positive picture from their other findings.

Jim remembered the phrase: "You're only as good as your last gig," It was, he considered, often the quote of macho management and people with selective memories, but all too often passive-aggressively trotted out when referring to C-SOC.

Jim called his team leaders together and began,

"Look, Amanda Driscoll has just visited us. She wants us to come up with something positive. Once again, we are under threat. It's our friend Bernard Driscoll that is turning the screws."

Marcus and the other team leaders looked at one another. They also realised that this was yet another play to try to get their group shot down.

Marcus was the first to comment, "I'd have thought that Driscoll would have been more interested in promoting our corner rather than trying to shut us down? Surely the fact that we can resolve more situations than much larger organisations across the river and in Cheltenham must count for something?"

Jim replied, "No, Driscoll doesn't see it like that. We have to do what Driscoll and SI6 say," he said. "Without their support, we are anyway in a difficult position."

"Amanda Miller, from SI6, and I go back a long way, and I'm sure she will do what she can to support us, but Driscoll is a different kettle of fish. He is all about power and also his own protection. He'll rattle on about protecting the civilian population but most of all he is trying to cover his own arse."

"So, did you learn anything new from Amanda Miller?" asked Marcus.

"No, she was really only able to tell us the same information that we already knew," said Jim.

"Did you mention anything about currency manipulation?" asked Marcus.

Jim looked quizzical.

"You know, the possible impact of cyber currency in the mix?" continued Marcus.

Jim looked at Marcus.

"You'd better brief me about that," he said.

"Okay," said Marcus, realising his original paper had failed to make any impact.

"Maybe I can see you about this after the main session? I think it is significant," continued Marcus.

Rosie looked towards Tyler. They both realised that they had a more complete picture of events in their team than the big bosses. Probably than Amanda Miller across at SI6.

The extractor

Marcus walked back to Rosie and Tyler.

"If the bombs don't get us, then the politicians will!" said Rosie.

Marcus nodded.

Then Rosie said to Marcus, "This is ridiculous - we seem to have found out more about the whole situation than anyone else, and there's only three of us in this sub-team."

Marcus replied," Yes, I agree, but the trouble is we will still need to substantiate everything we say. The reason there are so many people in those other departments is because of the burden of proof. It is why they spend so much time pulling their cases together. Politicians get easily bent out of shape if there is a chance of a diplomatic incident falling out of whatever we've identified."

Tyler asked, "Have we managed to get anywhere, identifying these two persons of interest?"

Rosie replied, "Hmm, the AI sifting technology still has a way to go.

"We still don't have any identification for the guy who we suspect as being the driver of the original bomb vehicle, but we did have some luck with the woman. It turns out that she is attached to the Russian embassy as a trade delegate.

"Of course, this is a cover, and her real purpose is to extract both the drivers from the scene completely," smiled Rosie.

"Okay, what do we have on this woman?" asked Marcus.

Well, we have a name - Alya Sokolov - and also the rather simple back story of her as an adviser but nothing else.

"Bird of prey?" mused Marcus, "That's what Sokolov means." Tyler and Rosie remembered that Marcus spoke Russian.

"Has she ever turned up in any other situations?" asked Marcus.

"Nothing that we have been able to identify so far," said Rosie. "Yet she does appear to have been in the UK for several weeks, with a side visit to France."

"This is still our best break so far with this," said Marcus," We now have a source that links back to the bombing and a trail that leads towards the Russians."

"Agreed," said Rosie," Although even at this stage, I'm still suspicious about what has actually taken place."

Marcus took a look at the photographs and the video that they had obtained.

"There's something that doesn't look quite the same between the two appearances of the guy," said Marcus, "I think we should run some more analysis of the video from inside the hotel."

"It's not very specific," said Matt, "But the guy in the second series of videos looks as if he is walking slightly differently from the guy who went into the hotel."

"Well, for a start, he's got his arm around the woman," said Rosie, "Or actually now you mention it, I think it's the other way around."

"If you look carefully, the woman seems to be guiding the guy towards the taxi."

Rosie wound the recording back and looked again, and sure enough, the man was looking a little the worse for wear in the second set of videos. It looked as if something had happened to him on the way through the hotel.

"Hotel bars can have that effect on me, too," commented Tyler.

"It looks as if he's been drugged or something," said Rosie looking more carefully at the video this time.

"Exactly," said Marcus, "Either drugged or perhaps damaged in some other way?"

"I think we could be witnessing the removal of our single direct link to the bombing," said Marcus. He looked grimly towards Rosie," I wonder if the woman has been sent to act as a disposal agent for the bomber.?"

Tyler was dialling up a Google maps view of the location that had been the final destination for the couple.

"We don't have any camera access unless any of the shops have rear-facing security cameras."

They traced the route back to a nearby side street. The street led in one direction to a dead end where a road had been blocked to prevent a rat run, and in the other direction, back onto one of the main thoroughfares.

"Okay." said Marcus, "We need to check the timings for vehicles entering and leaving this access road on the date in question."

"Oh, and we must wonder whether the exit was with the suspected bomber still alive," said Marcus.

PART TWO

Alya

Belladonna, n.: In Italian a beautiful lady; in English a deadly poison.

A striking example of the essential identity of the two tongues.

Ambrose Bierce

American Economics

Rosie noticed Marcus's expression.

"Hey, Marcus," what's the matter?"

"Well," he replied, "I miscalculated."

Rosie looked surprised. Marcus. The machine. Miscalculated. It did not compute.

"Okay, Marcus, you'll have to say more than that."

"I didn't realise that the follow-on paper to the one I wrote about the rouble was also significant," he began.

"What second paper?" asked Rosie. Tyler looked intrigued.

"Well, I wrote a second briefing paper. It was, how shall I say, more critical of our allies. Especially the Americans."

"What is it about?" asked Tyler, "More on the rouble?"

"Not exactly," said Marcus, "It's more of a multi-spectrum economic warfare piece."

"It's critical of our allies because, beyond the rouble concept, it looks as if the USA is also conducting a clandestine economic war against Moscow."

"What, like sanctions?" asked Tyler.

"Sanctions would be more overt. Remember the trouble that Trump had every time he opened his mouth about sanctions against some country or another?"

"So, this is less of a blunt instrument?" asked Rosie.

"Yes, although it is therefore sophisticated," added Marcus.

"Ah, so Trump wouldn't have been able to handle it anyway?" asked Tyler.

"Think of it as a Colder War," said Marcus.

"When I was writing the first rouble analysis, I came across quite a lot of material and from multiple sources. There's a whole gamut of approaches being deployed including speculation, financial market manipulation, information stream interception, business conglomerate information hiding, social media misuse, basic hacking via the internet, misuse of Governmental agencies, shady diplomacy, and some suspicious major business agreements.

"Daily this struggle can be seen playing out on the airwaves, in the war theatres in Ukraine and the Middle East, through the statements and accusations of diplomats, and in the economic sphere.

"Additionally, the debates and questions on whether a new cold war—the Colder War—have emerged.

"You see, in Putin's Russia, the mentality of the Cold War never really died, it just went further underground.

"Turning the Soviet Union into fifteen republics was not enough for the US. The newly emergent Russian Federation had to be placated in their views.

"That's why energy and petro-politics have been a significant feature of this multi-spectrum war too.

"Energy prices are a factor in this struggle, heavily linked to financial markets and national currencies. The manipulated decline in energy prices driven by flooding the global market with oil has augmented manipulation of the value of the rouble.

"Frankly, Saudi Arabia has also been a player, but Putin's Russia has known how to quietly take advantage of the situation.

"Unlike the USA with its incursions to Iraq and Iran?" asked Tyler.

"Yes, America has been wrong-footed in this, thinking that the Federation was about to call 'Game Over.' It soon realised that it would need to counter what the combined Russian Federation was doing. America then decided to run a two-pronged attack on the Russian Federation to cut Russia's revenues through market manipulation via economic sanctions and price drops.

"So, the rouble manipulation started in the USA?" asked Tyler.

"You bet it did," said Marcus, unusually intense," If the Americans hadn't started to play around with currency to try to drag Russia down, then I doubt Russia would have thought of its own currency manipulation."

"It's copycat," said Rosie, "Like the space race. The difference is that the Russians might really have something this time, instead of just poorly engineered copies of what the Americans have done"

"That's right," said Marcus," And the Russians can set up large click farms to manipulate the internet. They can keep them stealthy and undetected."

"I suppose if the Americans tried this, there would be a reporter on the doorstep in a few minutes," said Tyler.

'Ah, yes, the free press," replied Marcus.

"So, by imposing sanctions on the Russian economy, the US and its allies, including Australia, Canada, the European Union and Japan can drive offensives against Russia's leading source of revenue — energy. That has knocked the rouble and accounts for part of the reason Russia may have been driving the price.

Marcus looked at Rosie and Tyler. They were processing what he was saying.

"So, the reason that Russia may have got into the fake money business might be because of what the Americans have been doing?" asked Tyler.

"Maybe," said Marcus. "It's a strange form of cause and effect. Remember this is supposition by me. I've written this up but kept it away from official channels up to now. The materials I've used to create the positioning are from public domain sources, so I'm not breaking any confidential barriers. However, once I've assembled the story, it is somewhat incendiary."

"It's also somewhat bizarre," said Rosie, "Because it shows that an American plot to weaken Russia may have backfired spectacularly."

"There's at least a couple of big problems here," said Marcus.

Rosie replied, "First, if this is true and came to light, it would massively discredit America. Secondly, the way that Russia appears to be manufacturing the fake currency suggests a massive hole in cryptographic systems. It doesn't seem possible that it could be so easy for a Nation-State to be able to print fake money."

"Agreed," said Marcus. "And it looks as if this started some time ago, maybe as a result of the first rouble price drop back in 2014 - although the original system would have taken years to gear up."

Tyler asked," You'll have to explain."

"Well, back in 2014, Interfax's Vyacheslav Terekhov commented on the rouble currency crisis to Russian President Vladimir Putin during a Kremlin press conference. He said something about being in the midst of a deep currency crisis, one that even Central Bank employees say they could not have foreseen in their worst nightmares.

"Putin went on to explain that the situation has changed under the influence of certain foreign economic factors, primarily the price of energy resources, of oil and consequently of gas as well. He didn't go all out to say it was the Americans, but everyone knew what he was thinking."

"That the Americans were manipulating currencies to drag the Russian economy down?" said Rosie.

Marcus answered, "I guess that Putin sanctioned the original project to create market manipulation as a counter to what the United States and its allies were doing.

"Somebody smart would have come forward with a proposition. Only a few people understood cryptocurrency internals at that time, although plenty of people - including Tyler and his friend Matt - would have the capability to be able to mine the currency.

"I think Matt was smarter than that," said Tyler," He seemed to know about the innards of the various systems as well."

"Surely the Treasury and the FCA would pick up on this?" asked Tyler.

"Yes, they did at the time, and there was quite extensive coverage in the financial press. The Economist even wrote a leader article about it. But there was also a lot of other stuff happening, so although it continued to be extensively reported on media like Russia Today, it was less well-analysed in the UK and American press. We were all more interested in the price of oil in the way that it affected petrol for cars and heating for homes and industry. The usual vagueness descended over much of what was happening."

Rosie smiled," Yes, the way that the press doesn't analyse the impacts and reasons, more that it re-sprays the press releases and other guff that the PR teams create."

"So, Marcus, is it time to bring forward your paper about this," asked Tyler, "There's already plenty here, and you seem to still be adding to it."

"I guess so, although the original reason I was working on this secretively, was because of what happened with the 'rouble' paper as it moved up the chain. I started to get a sense that it wasn't being treated at the appropriate level of its security clearance."

"In other words, it was being leaked?" asked Rosie.

"Leaked, along with me as the author, which is something we are not supposed to ever do," said Marcus. "I'm all for rightful credit, but when it's something potentially incendiary, the anonymity and the confidentiality help to protect us."

Marcus continued, "Some smart analysts said that the drop in the Russian rouble's value was a result of the market acting on its own. I didn't buy that. It's increasingly difficult to prove what has been happening with all the microtransactions that nowadays take place by a computer algorithm in the trading desks.

"Only a few people pointed toward market manipulation, and they were looking toward Russia rather than anything that the

Americans might have been doing.

"That's what made the whole operation so brilliant in its early stages. American finds a way to tweak Russia's currency to produce an economic advantage. Then Russia discovers it and takes the original idea in a whole new direction. Still using the cover of micropayments and microtransactions to shield and diffuse what has been happening.

"That's how I originally started to look at the way that Russia seemed to be holding the rouble price from their own manipulations. The more obvious move was to blame it on the Russian government and Vladimir Putin. That's what led me to the idea there might be new money involved in the process.

"My second paper goes on to say it is not merely a result of the market acting on its own or the result of Kremlin-style policies.

"If the US had been making a Colder War play, then its objectives and policy would deliberately target Russia for destabilisation and devastation. It would be something cooked up below the Presidential level though, for fear of it being accidentally blurted or tweeted into the world."

Tyler and Rosie both grinned.

"It might have been initially a US plot to bring about Russian currency and economic instability, but it could easily have a knock-on effect across to the EU and other markets.

"Of course, the US would have been in control of what was happening until Russia switched on its money printing press. Russia would have needed leverage to fight back, and I guess that is when they moved across into cyber currency.

"Some economists in the US must be wondering what the hell they've done if they have continued to monitor outcomes," said Rosie.

"They know for sure," said Marcus," But I don't think they are asking questions about it."

"Not until they have erected the Teflon walls?" asked Rosie.

"Yes," said Marcus, "Otherwise, it will spark major international rows in all directions."

"That's where the Kremlin has been clever. Instead of depleting their foreign currency reserves and gold holdings of the Russian Federation, they've turned to faking money."

"In a way, it's a brilliant plan.," gasped Rosie.

Marcus continued, "As an example, Putin is on record as saying that the Russian government and Russian Central Bank should not hand out gold and foreign currency reserves or burn them on the market, but instead provide lending resources.

"That was a clever smokescreen for cyber currency injections. If the Kremlin knows what Washington was doing, then better to play along with it.

"Frankly, the US was replaying some of its old Cold War game plans against Russia.

"All the moving pieces around energy price manipulation, the currency devaluation, and even US attempts to entrap Russia in a conflict with its sister-republic Ukraine are all replays of US tactics that have been used before during the Cold War.

Rosie chipped in: "So dragging Russia into Ukraine is like a replay of how the US dragged the Soviet Union into Afghanistan previously?"

Marcus continued, "Yes, and the manipulation of energy prices and currency markets parallels the US strategy used to weaken Iraq, Iran, and the Soviet Union during the Afghan-Soviet War and Iran War.

"Instead of trying to stop the value of the rouble from dropping, the Kremlin appears to have decided to strategically invest in Russia's internal capital, using foreign exchange. It can do this with blended money. Mix real money and some of the fake money created through the cyber-fraud. They created a working framework for what is effectively massive nation-state money laundering.

Tyler looked at Marcus, "So where, exactly, is your second paper right now?"

Rosie was thinking about another cigarette when the phone rang. It was James.

"Bingo," he said.

"How so, James? "

"The AI system worked. We've got a positive identification of your bomber. Or should I say, your bomber's accomplice? We ran your two pictures through a few systems, and it spotted this person coming to the UK about a couple of months ago. Then leaving for CDG and then returning a couple of days later."

"And her name is Alya Sokolov," said James, "A full-fledged Russian agent. B-INNG-Go!"

"James, that's brilliant! Thank you so much,"

"The data files are winging their way across to you, as we speak, but I thought I'd like to tell you in person! Hey, Alya is badass. You take care now," he added," Love and kisses!"

"James, Ruck on!" said Rosie as the call cleared.

Rework

Marcus said," I'm going to get a cleaned-up copy of my report. The version I have on my secure machine back at the hotel includes the external references I used when I was compiling it."

"Before I head over there, I will speak to Jim about getting access to information about this woman Alya."

"I think Jim will have the right access into SI6 to help us with this."

"I'll see you both tomorrow with my updated version of the report," he added, "and we will need to manage the circulation extremely carefully."

Marcus crossed the corridor and tapped the door to Jim's office.

Jim looked up as Marcus entered, "There's been a development on the bombing," said Marcus, "I think I have the first positive lead relating to who may be behind it."

"We tracked the bomber across London, and he went into a hotel and later appeared with someone who we believe to be a Russian agent." said Marcus," I need a way to track her down and potentially stop her from leaving the country."

"We have a name - Alya Sokolov, which we obtained via the normal routes," said Marcus.

"The thing is, she's unknown to us and therefore not in our systems. We've some basic data that Rosie has acquired from Ops. Security, but it's not like a full agent profile."

"You'd better get into a position that helps you to follow her then," said Jim.

"I can arrange something for you via border control. You'll have to send over the documentation that you do hold. We will also need to tell Amanda Miller at MI6 that we are doing this."

"That way we can expedite this whole process," Jim looked up towards Marcus, "good work Marcus," he said," This is the first proper lead we've found."

"The people from GCHQ and SI6 haven't given us anything new, and the police are only helpful concerning the cloned plates on the taxi.

"We both know that the car is otherwise clean, and we won't get anything further from it.

"Except," said Marcus, "The make of the explosive, of course."

Marcus made his way back to the hotel. He had much to prepare for the morning.

Sokolov

Another rainy day as Tyler arrived at the office. Rosie was studying a report.

"Is that the new report from Marcus?" asked Tyler.

"No," said Rosie "it's the report that Marcus wrote previously. The one about the currency management of the rouble."

"Marcus must have worked late because he was not answering his phone when I tried to raise him this morning," she continued, "I'll give him until ten, and then I'll try contacting him again,"

Tyler decided he would also re-read the report from Marcus. He noticed it now had all of the security classification markings on it that showed it as a high-status document.

Just before 10 o'clock, there was a phone call to Rosie.

Others had been trying to contact Marcus but been referred operationally across to Rosie instead. This call was from Jim, who was only a couple of offices away.

"That person of interest that Marcus described to me yesterday," said Jim, "Alya Sokolov."

"The border controls have managed to stop her. We all assumed she would make her way out through one of the airports, perhaps even by a small plane to get across into mainland Europe.

"To our great surprise, she decided instead to use St Pancras station and to go across on the Eurostar."

"It was an easy option that would normally avoid detection, but luckily we had an alert set at the border. Sokolov is now being held by the local border control unit. They have put her into a secure location temporarily. Until we can request access to question her."

"The difficulty is, Marcus did talk about this with Amanda, which means that SI6 have asked for first access. We can probably go across and sit in on the interview, but they won't release her to us until they have questioned her."

"This is something to do with Driscoll again. I think he is trying to prove a point by only using the big departments to manage the situation," said Tyler.

"I doubt whether he is even aware that we were the people who identified her as a person of interest."

Tyler replaced the receiver and said to Rosie, "We must contact Marcus now."

Rosie nodded. "You know what," she said," I think we should head over to the hotel, and we can discuss this with Marcus there."

"If he's had a hard night working, then it is a good place for us to refuel him with some decent coffee as well."

Tyler grinned, "Yes, good idea."

They were out in the air for a few minutes. A crisp day on the way back to the hotel. A quick pit-stop at the adjacent Starbucks.

As they entered the hotel, Tyler could see that there was additional security.

Both plainclothes and also limited uniformed police were now inside the hotel.

Rosie was smiled at by one of the policemen who recognised her as a guest.

Not the same for Tyler, who was stopped and questioned before he was allowed into the elevator.

"Wow", said Tyler, "That was quite strict. If you hadn't been with me, I doubt whether I would have been able to get into the lift."

"It's nice to know they are looking after us well," said Rosie as they made their way to the 6th floor.

"I'm on the seventh, actually," said Rosie, "It's amusing that they've given me the executive floor while Marcus is on one of the normal floors. I think we both have pretty similar rooms, although we also both have access to the executive lounge in any case."

"One of the perks of Grade 7," said Tyler, "I'm not bitter," smiling as they tapped the door to Marcus's room.

There was a long pause and no answer.

Rosie picked up her cell phone and called Marcus.

She could hear the phone ringing from inside the room. "There's no response from Marcus," said Rosie.

Tyler ventured, "He's probably taking a shower; let's try the house phone."

Rosie picked up on the quaver in Tyler's voice.

Tyler found a wall phone and called down to the reception and asked to be connected to Marcus's room by the switchboard. Rosie pressed her ear to the door and could hear the other room phone ringing.

Still no sign of Marcus. "Okay," said Rosie, "I think we need to get the security guys to let us into the room."

She walked back to the lift area, where one of the security men was standing.

"We need to get access to room 6507," said Rosie, "Our colleague is supposed to be at an important meeting now."

They once again showed their passes to the security guard and he, in turn, called to someone else. Within seconds two extra people had appeared.

One was in full military combat clothes. The other was probably a soldier in civilian clothing but carrying a master key.

"Okay, we are going to open the room," said the uniformed soldier. "But we will enter before you do in case there is anything unusual. Be vigilant and be careful, " he added.

The soldier approached the door, and the man with the security card pressed it gently onto the lock.

The door immediately clicked to green so that the room could be entered. The soldier held up a shield and then pushed gently against the door.

It opened quietly into the room, and as they looked past the shield, they could see there was no sign of habitation. The room was made up as if it had been set by the housekeeping staff, everything was in its place and on the small desk table was Marcus's phone. There was no sign of Marcus. One of the soldiers pushed into the side door, which led to the en-suite shower and bathroom.

"Clear," he said. The other soldier nodded they were also looking around the room for other signs of unusual devices; altogether, they spent around three minutes before they would let Tyler and Rosie into the room.

"Okay, we have checked the room, and it appears to be secured," said the first soldier.

"There's no one in here, and it doesn't look as if it has been slept in," said the second soldier.

Tyler and Rosie looked around.

They could see that everything was very tidy.

"No laptop, just the charger," said Tyler to Rosie.

"Marcus's phone is here," said Rosie.

"Yes, it's his office phone. I can't see his personal one, though."

"If he had taken his office phone, we would have been able to easily track him."

Tyler nodded," I wonder whether Marcus has simply gone home?"

Marcus and Rosie looked at one another. Neither of them believed that Marcus would be at home. Something else had happened.

Marcus was missing.

Cutouts

Jim took a cab from Earls Court to the building close to SI6 headquarters where Alya was detained.

Amanda Miller was already there, and they were ready to begin Alya's questioning.

Jim was officially only present as an observer and had to stay in a separate room with video camera and audio feeds from the interrogation area.

The interrogation room was a blue-painted room with just a chair, a table and a wall-mounted camera and several ceiling-mounted microphones. Around the edge of the wall ran a panic bar at about chest height.

Jim admired it for the theatre. He knew they could as easily have conjured up a comfy living room with sofas and chintzy curtains.

There were two guards placed inside the room, one male and one female with Alya seated on the chair with her hands secured by a chain connected to the table.

The lead interrogator was female as Amanda watched from the observation room.

"Not interrogating, then?" asked Jim.

"They are the professionals," replied Amanda. She was pleased enough to be outside of the room.

"It's also more secure to not have the suspect able to identify either of us," murmured Amanda.

"No, we'll leave that for Bernard," said Jim.

They both sniggered.

The questioning began routinely enough, establishing Alya's name, her back story, and her reason for being in the United Kingdom.

Alya said that she was a secretary from the Russian Embassy and that there was no right for the UK to detain her.

Alya recognised she was being held by a part of the secret services, although there was nothing on their clothing or other forms of formal identification.

"Why am I being held…This is against the law. Your law. You cannot hold me without reason. I must contact my Embassy. I need to make a phone call."

The first thing that Amanda noticed was that the identity of Alya was a close match for the formal photographs and passes that had been provided by border control. She also noticed how Alya spoke excellent English and would have placed her as a typical well-heeled South Londoner, maybe from somewhere like Wimbledon.

She didn't give off an assassin vibe.

Next, Amanda noted Alya's physical appearance. Here things didn't seem quite right. She was slightly different from the pictures. Alya was wiry and slim. She looked like she worked out and had well-defined muscles in her arms and across her body.

This Alya was a little more curvaceous. Amanda didn't think she'd be able to run a fast 2km, while the Alya in the pictures most certainly could.

The interrogators continued, although there was a limit to their knowledge.

Alya quickly realised this and was not forthcoming.

"Jim, I don't think it is her," said Amanda.

Jim nodded agreement, "I was beginning to wonder what was wrong. The answers are evasive but show a lack of knowledge rather than a deliberate attempt to send us in the wrong direction."

"For example, that question about her family; You'd think she would mention her sister, even when we have told her we know about the sister."

"Yes, but she couldn't say what colour hair, or the sister's birthday. This wasn't supposed to be the tough part of the interrogation."

There was a buzz. A red light flashed in the interrogation suite.

"They are coming out, "said Amanda, "Let's ask them what they think."

The two interrogators stood and walked outside of the room. A few minutes later, they entered the viewing booth.

"It is strange," said one of the interrogators, "She is either very good, or there is something else going on."

"She doesn't seem to know anything, not even her own family history," said the second interrogator, "It's as if we have been given a substitute."

"A cutout? A cutout of the cutout?" asked Amanda.

"It's a clever move if that is what they have done. We've stood down the border controls, and yet we have possibly the wrong person in detention."

"Bernard will love this," muttered Jim to Amanda.

"I agree," said Amanda. What about the passport biometrics?

"I'll get our people to take a look. Maybe they've been doctored."

"It's becoming more commonplace now," said one of the interrogators, "We had a Russian chap in here a couple of weeks ago. Positively identified from his passport but in reality, nothing like his pictures. Someone has got hold of the encoders."

"Let's think about this for a minute," said Jim, "Would it be better for the Russians to think we have not realised their deception?"

"Good point," said Amanda. She looked at the two interrogators.

They looked at one another.

"Yes, we get it, you want us to continue routinely for a few more hours. We had to do something similar to the Russian man a few weeks ago."

"Meanwhile, we need to send out the alert to Borders again," said Jim.

Amanda nodded, "So what shall we tell Driscoll?"

"Tell him it is proving difficult to get information even with two of the most highly skilled interrogators."

They chuckled.

Jim's phone rang. It was Rosie from the office.

"Jim? There's been a development."

"Okay, just one minute," he replied.

He stepped out into the corridor.

"Go ahead,"

"We have been running some image software to cross-check people at the Russian Embassy. There are around 15 people there that roughly match Alya Sokolov's picture. We dug a bit deeper through the profiling.

"Here's what we found: This one: Katarina. She looks like Alya and has a comprehensive travel profile. She has been in several countries and we have her marked down as a frontline operative under challenging situations. She has been through military training and has a reputation as a suspected sniper and assassin.

The file also goes on to describe her as a fixer. I've sent the record across to your phone.

Jim looked at the record. It certainly looked like Alya.

He stepped back into the viewing room.

"Amanda, I think this might be Alya."

Amanda studied the pictures on Jim's phone.

Yes, the correct build, the right facial profile.

"Unfortunately, the surveillance team reckon there are around 15 women who approximate Alya's appearance," said Jim.

"They've not been searching sexy Russian brides, have they?" joked Amanda.

"No, but I can see their point with Alya," said Jim.

"Or Katarina," said Amanda, "Katarina Voronin."

"Katarina Voronin?" answered Jim, "Things just got serious. She is a Russian agent we have been tracking for years." She pops up from time to time, in places where there is some kind of mayhem.

Jim picked up his phone and called Rosie, "Hi Rosie, I think we've just found Katarina Voronin. She's popped up cross-referenced to Alya Sokolov."

"What, as an associate?" asked Rosie

"No, as the self-same person, we think the Alya we are holding is a case of mistaken identity."

"Voronin is top league," said Rosie, "Security services have been tracking her around for years. I'll try to pull off her data."

A few minutes later, an email arrived for Jim on his phone.

"Here we are," he said

"She has been trained by the FSB and has spent time in Germany, Austria, France, and the United Kingdom. It says she is fluent in German, French and English as well as her native Russian.

"There's a trail of coincidences associated with her time in various countries. A bombing in Amsterdam, the assassination of a Russian banker in Turkey, gun-running across the Belgian border. A huge bank heist in Austria using an armoured car.

"The links we show illustrate that she might just have popped into these countries from one of her home ones. And each time it is just around when the event took place.

"I'm not sure that I'd call it a weak link but look, she has a child still in Moscow.

"By my reckoning, the boy is around two years old now. It also looks to me as if most of Katerina's work stopped around two years ago.

"It implies that she has been retired from the field."

"But, presumably brought back for this job?" summarised Jim.

"Let's ask "Alya" about her little boy…" said Jim.

He flipped the interrogation button and saw the interrogators pause. One got up and left the room.

Jim walked into the corridor and talked to the interrogator.

"Okay, the question is primed, let's see what happens next!"

Sure enough, the interrogators asked the question. The reaction was remarkable. Alya replied but in her reply said, 'You keep my children out of this."

"Children," said Jim.

"Children," replied Amanda, "We've been played."

"But they don't know how much we have found out."

Jim travelled back across London to his base office.

Now that Marcus had disappeared there was an increased risk to his other team members.

He'd have to move them to somewhere less public. The catalogue of problems was rising.

Two bombs, a banker's disappearance, Marcus disappearance, the mystery bombers, the Russian woman. Currency manipulation. Somehow, he would have to make sense of all of this. That's where he'd usually rely upon Marcus to bring together the most likely theory.

Instead, he had to ship Tyler and Rosie to yet another centre of operations.

He entered their office. They both looked up.

"Anything useful from the Russian?" asked Tyler.

"Only that she is a substitute, to throw us off the track of the real Alya Sokolov."

"Now, I've been thinking, and I need you two to move your centre of operation…To GCHQ."

Tyler thought about it, "Finally, a chance to stay in a hotel on the department's budget."

Rosie thought about what she'd needed to tell Vanessa. Things had been trying over the last few days, with Rosie mysteriously staying away but not allowed to explain anything specific to Vanessa.

"When are we going?" Asked Rosie.

"Tomorrow," answered Jim, "It'll give you time to pack."

Driscoll on TV

After Bernard Driscoll's morning television interview, there had been something of a backlash.

Despite his attempts to show that he was on top of the bombings and had excellent support, the allegations were now that he was running an outfit that was unfit for purpose.

It was what he had intended in one way, but the big fingers were now pointing back directly to him. He was considered to be part of the problem rather than the solution.

His advisors suggested he should appear in a few more interviews, the next one being a radio interview.

"Thank you, Minister, for agreeing to appear on the World at Midday. Minister, you've already implied that your own systems and services need some kind of update. What are your plans now to prevent further disruption and damage to London and potentially even loss of life?

"This is beginning to look more like the period in the 70s when there were concerted bombing campaigns across London. Surely with today's modern technologies and surveillance, you would be better able to predict and pre-empt such events?

Driscoll was prepared for this, " But first let me say that we are doing everything to stem the flow of such terrorist atrocities. "We have already increased the boots on the ground support in the London area. In practice, we think that these attacks may have been specifically aimed at two of our own buildings.

"That's what you said on the previous television interview Minister. That you were running operations from these two buildings."

"Is it possible, then, that the attacks were aimed at yourselves? And isn't that quite worrying that your own systems are unable even to detect direct attacks on your own environments.?"

Driscoll again: "We've seen the government's priorities around these matters change over the last few years. Our predecessors diluted the effect of our spending by adding in these new departments, with the result resources are spread more thinly. We are now in the process of re-consolidating so that we have a better and more critical mass where we need it".

"We're going now to our security specialist, Dr Stannard, based in the University of Manchester to ask for his thoughts on the current situation. Good Morning, Dr Stannard,"

"Good morning to everyone. Yes, we have monitored the last few years of GCHQ MI6 MI5 and these other smaller departments and have noticed one particular aspect. Usually, intelligence is only gathered after significant events rather than before them.

"The security services, with a few exceptions, have been very unsuccessful at predicting most of the big events that have occurred.

"Let's look at some track record. Aside from the two recent bombing attempts there have been situations in the past.

"The lack of identification of a significant number of terrorists that have lived in the United Kingdom before moving to other countries where they have laid bombs or created different types of disruption.

"The firebombing in the United Kingdom of several notable buildings.

"The hacking of government Department secure files, the denial of service attacks on several UK corporations, the uploading into visible parts of the Internet of various forms of secured information including the source code for the systems software on one of our nuclear plants.

"These are all examples over the last three or four years.

"While it's fair to say that financial policies changed for funding of some of these departments, most of this has happened within the current government's reign."

"Minister?"

"Let me be clear: Of course, we are unable to make changes to funding policies in a matter of moments. Look: All of these require careful consideration and have had to go through various Treasury committees in order to make the changes. That's one of the reasons why I use these current examples as a way to expedite the changes that we think we need, since the last government were in power."

"But surely over the last year or so that was a fairly substantial increase, a doubling no less, of the funding available to the central security agencies? Are you saying that this was still not sufficient?"

"It's not simply a matter of funding per se," answered the Minister, "it's also a question of allocations and where they are placed. We need to ensure that the right people get the funding."

Dr Stannard interrupted, "This is all so much political posturing. You are trying to cover up for an extensive and very bureaucratic system that is too stodgy to be able to react to the type of circumstances that we see now with modern terrorism. Whether it's terrorism or just cranks, you seem to be always running to catch up.

"The very idea that you are now somehow able to monitor everything that is happening stinks. You can't just track everything and hope to find the right answers.

"Let's be truthful about this; it's only when you have tipoffs that you even stand a chance to be able to find out things in advance.

The Minister looked a little flustered but decided to bluster his way out of it," You are oversimplifying this Dr Stannard, "he said, "A whole intelligence ecosystem is a very finely tuned machine.

"We are not working on this alone. We are also working with our allies in NATO and also with the Americans."

Dr Stannard interrupted, "Yes, but it's not a big secret that you don't like to share too much with, for example, the Americans. Even when you say that you are working closely together, there is usually some reluctance to divulge more than is absolutely necessary?"

"That's simply not true," said the Minister," We have a strong relationship with both the Americans and our NATO allies across Europe. We share information on a regular and routine basis."

The interviewer cut in," Okay, let's move this along, shall we? We need to understand what are the concrete steps now, Minister, to alleviate the current situation?"

Bernard Driscoll replied," I'm sure you understand that I am not really in a position to directly answer that. This is all a matter of national security, and we are in the middle of a delicate phase. It would be counter-productive for me to tell you too much about what is going on. Please rest assured that the highest priorities are being given to handling the current situation."

"Thank you, Minister, and now it's time for the weather."

Amanda winced as she listened to the broadcast. She knew that Driscoll was prone to bluster his way out of situations, and this was yet another example. Amanda was sure that this would not go down well in the shortened news clips that would undoubtedly follow. Unfortunately, this was the second major interview that the Minister had produced in such a style, and she was reasonably sure that his days were now numbered.

Her phone rang; it was Jim.

"I guess you just listened to that interview?" he asked.

"Yes, not so much world at midday as the world at a loss," she replied, " That was not a good interview for the Minister."

"The problem I see now," said Jim, "is that he is quite likely to lash out before he is replaced. We will need to be careful over the next 24 hours that he does not do anything stupid."

"I think we should probably keep the silent running that we have established for the little project in Cheltenham." replied Amanda.

"I agree," said Jim.

Country Cousins

Lists only spell out the things that can be taken away from us by moths and rust and thieves.

If something is valuable, don't put it in a list. Don't even say the words.

Douglas Coupland

GCHQ

Tyler entered the GCHQ briefing room. He'd expected it to be busier. It was a small auditorium, suited for the briefing of maybe 60 people.

There were 6 people present.

A woman stepped forward — long dark hair with a hint of greying, a plain black T-shirt and jeans.

"Welcome to GCHQ," she said, "My name is Grace Fielding.

"I've been assigned as the project manager for this next operation - it's called 'Mynah Bird'."

"That will confuse everyone on the misspellings," thought Tyler.

"We'll all introduce ourselves in a moment but for the two people from London please could you raise hands and just show the others who you are.

"These are Tyler and Rosie,"

"They were working closely with Marcus and are the basis for the discovery. They were directly involved in the development of the rouble manipulation theory through the use of cyber currency.

"Our job is to figure out a way to stealthily end what the Russians have been doing."

"But does that mean we are going to try to hack the Russians?" asked one of the GCHQ people.

"That's right, Daniel," said Grace.

"But we think they are using server farms and click farms," said another of the GCHQ contingent, "They seem to be based in multiple cities too: Kazan, Chelyabinsk, Omsk, Samara and Rostov-on-Don, and more…"

"That's right," said Grace," We'll need some smart methods to put this genie back in the bottle."

"Marcus Barton produced this report which you have all read now, which explains the surmised basis for cyber manipulation."

"We think it was this report which caused him to be taken away from his hotel room by, as yet, unknown people."

"Other presumptive events lead us to think that it is the Russians that have done this. This is not for circulation or discussion outside of this base. I'm going to hand over now to Tyler Sloan, to take us through the system."

Tyler started to explain the cyber mining system used by the Russians.

"I assume that's why we this project is called Mynah Bird?" he said, "Because the cybercash system mimics the real one?"

Then he described the ability to use the mined coins in a blend with other currencies to create new forms of financial instrument which could be used for routine trading and in effect to be used to balance the cost the exchange rate of the rouble.

"So, it becomes a way to secretly print vast quantities of foreign exchange currency in a state-sponsored exercise," he concluded.

Grace took over, "We also picked up on this via a major Bank's London trading desks, and I think it was Marcus Barton's team that were involved directly in this disclosure."

"Indeed, the source of the main derivative trading - Victor Boyd - head of group trading - has also disappeared. It's like the links to this are being systematically removed."

"We have brought Tyler and Rosie down to GCHQ to protect themselves from whatever has happened to Marcus."

Rosie and Tyler looked at one another. They had not been told this vital detail.

"They were secretly brought to GCHQ, and only the people in this room and a few senior staff know anything about this."

Tyler raised his hand. Grace looked towards him," Yes? A question?"

"That's right," said Tyler, "My concern is that when we were in the Earls Court building and even before that when we were still in St Martins-le-Grand, there was some kind of leak. In other words, the bombings have been following us.

"Our supposition is that the bombs created a diversion which pushed Marcus and our team into the secured hotel."

"That would have made a pre-planned raid on the hotel possible," continued Tyler.

"I've seen the briefing from Jim Cavendish about this. He was part of the interrogation of the Russian fixer woman who is still being held by SI6".

"Yes, but we know that she was a substitute?" chipped in Rosie.

"Agreed," said Grace, "We are still working to detain the real fixer, Alya Sokolov, also known as Katarina Voronin."

"And it looks as if the stakes were high because we believe her last role was to dispose of the two bombers to remove them from the chain of investigation."

"Do we think that the Russian organised crime is also involved with this?" asked one of the GCHQ people.

There was a small giggle around the auditorium.

"Quite likely, the government to organised crime area is quite a grey area. We know that there is a very porous line between the Russian government and the Russian organised crime syndicates."

"So, follow the money," said Rosie, "That's what Marcus would say."

"Good point," said Grace," starting from where."

"I'd think laterally about this," said Tyler," Ignore the main derivatives and their trades, instead look for any new large-scale gains by senior Russian officials."

"Yes, skimming the money from the top of the generated pile," said Rosie.

The GCHQ people nodded as she said this.

Grace smiled, "Yes, we are already doing that, as it happens; usually there's a leak somewhere. This time it is a member of the Russian Central Bank - Grigori Gulnik. He seems to have so much money that he's been sending some of it across to the Cayman Islands, for safe, tax-free keeping.

"Caymans?" said Rosie.

"Yes, it's a predictable destination of choice for Russian investors. Particularly Tier 1 investor visa Russians, who have a sort of free pass to London included with every deposit."

"Gulnik has bought a couple of homes in London. Both in the $20 million range. One of the purchases hardly trips the spending scales for Russian purchases in London. The second and his interest in a third property suggests a run rate of income that needs to be secured. Gulnik is trying to spread his risk around. He knows that if he leaves it in Russia, it could all be taken away from him by Putin's robbers."

"And Gulnik is a Turkish name, isn't it?" asked Rosie.

"It could be Turkish," agreed Grace, "But his nationality is given as Russian."

"Okay," said Grace, "In a minute we will take you through to the main operations room."

"We are in the inner ring of GCHQ, and now we are about to go underground into the tank. It will give us a chance to show you a few of the tunnels as well."

"It looks as if we are going to become cyber-hackers now," stated Rosie.

Tyler said: "We will need to use some of the same techniques that cyberterrorists deploy, to track down the Russian systems."

Grace added, "We had to do something similar when we were trying to figure out what ISIL was doing as it attempted to hack the power companies.

"It's no real secret that Islamic State was trying to hack US power companies. A section chief at the FBI's cyber division was first to draw it to attention, but claimed that they had, 'Strong intent but low capability.' He went on to say that they'd simply buy the capability."

"That's around when the US Justice Department started making arrests and charging individuals with providing material support to the Islamic State, computer hacking and identity theft.

"It was all in conjunction with the theft and release of personally identifiable information belonging to US service members and civilian government employees. The original data had been stolen from the servers of a US retail chain.

Daniel continued, "Hussain had tweeted in the name of the Islamic State Hacking Division a link to a 30-page document that contained the information allegedly stolen by the arrested hackers. I still have the text on my computer.

"To be honest, although having personal information or an email address published can be threatening and serve as an incredibly intimate invasion of privacy, it's not the real game. While such hacks are bothersome, they are not immediately deadly."

"Usually, the goal of cyber terrorists is to have the ability to conduct attacks that result in death or significant destruction — attacks that provoke terror — with just the stroke of a keyboard."

Tyler asked, "So the terrorist made as much as they could of a rather basic situation?"

Daniel interrupted: "Yes, and unwittingly gave away a show of their current capability. At the time, their published document threatened, let's see...

Daniel scrolled through a document on his PC.

"Here we are, Melodrama Central... 'we are in your emails and computer systems, watching and recording your every move, we have your names and addresses, we are in your social media accounts, we are extracting confidential data and passing on your personal information to the soldiers of the Khalifa, who soon with the permission of Allah will strike at your necks in your own lands!'

"The Khalifa refers to the Caliphate; You'll have seen this type of long-winded messaging on other recent hacks too."

Grace continued, "There's a couple of other points to this, though. The first is that although there was real data in play, it was quite opportunistic. Admittedly it was service personnel names, but really it was a lucky strike by the hackers."

"It was enough to be able to sell some credibility to the people who would pay them but not anywhere near good enough to do any real damage. Except to get Hussain killed by way of US retaliation of course.

"The second hidden fact is that the US then recruited the original hacker to in effect change sides and to work for them. It's a common enough situation and one where he could carry on with his hobby but now get paid by the Americans. For him, it wasn't so much about ideology as about greed. That and if he didn't comply, he'd be locked away forever.

"The incidents showed the intent of ISIL to develop a robust cyber warfare capability.

"It's been useful because we've had to keep up with the latest thinking here too. We don't have a US cyber hacker to throw at this (although we could probably get the Americans to chip in), but we do have our own improved capabilities."

"Why not simply go to the Americans for direct assistance?" Asked Tyler.

"We'd have to spill the beans on the rest of the situation if we did that," said Grace.

"The result would be that the Americans would want to take full control and move everything to Langley. We've seen it too many times before."

"I think there might be other reasons for keeping the Americans muted in this investigation," added Rosie, "Some of it is referred to in Marcus second paper."

Tyler nodded, and Grace looked intrigued.

Grace added, "For this, we'll use our own people, and if needed we normally would augment from the local market."

"I'm assuming you can't do that in this case?" asked Rosie. "Using experts from one of those small firms who claim specialised skills in all of this."

"We can't this time," said Grace, "This is far too sensitive, and if the Russians have figured out a way to manufacture fake blockchains then we need to shut it down, not provide tips on how to make it proliferate. We don't want economic warfare on the back of this."

"Well, not forgetting the real warfare with explosions that started off this chain of events!" said Tyler.

"I agree, and I'm sorry, I didn't mean to detract from the awful time you two have been having over the last few days," said Grace hastily.

"The other aspect of this is the use of state sponsorship," interrupted Daniel once more, "To date, the very few seriously destructive hacks we have seen have been conducted by state sponsors such as the authors of the Stuxnet malware."

Grace added, "Thanks, Daniel, Indeed, most private hackers seek money or thrills, and so they have not focused on cyber warfare — or more accurately, asymmetrical cyberterrorism — as much as they have cyber theft and cyber vandalism."

"So cyber warfare has mostly been the province of nation-states, and cybersecurity experts believe that wide-scale cyber warfare can be conducted only by national players.

"That is consistent with what the Russians appear to have been trying but is more covert even than a typical cyberterrorist based approach. There are a few nations out there who want to make their attacks look as if they have come from other places. In effect, state-sponsored attacks dressed up to look like cyberterrorists. Usually designed to look like small-timers as well."

Tyler interrupted, "That makes the cyber money situation very different. It's asymmetric, but with the huge advantage to the attacker."

Grace added, "Now the question becomes whether the perpetrators have developed something themselves or whether they have gone elsewhere to obtain the special software?"

Daniel added, "Normally, for routine malware attacks, the perpetrator can buy the malware from a commercial hacking crew and then repurpose it for a more malicious purpose than simply stealing."

"State sponsorship is also a potential way for terrorist actors to gain access to malware tools for asymmetrical cyber terrorist attacks," added Tyler.

"But It seems less likely that there would be a such a ready market for the mining software, or if there is then it has been very well-concealed, certainly from us, and we were in the exact market," Tyler added.

"It would need to have been very well-concealed," said Daniel.

Tyler started, "You may already know that I was part of a small cyber mining team right up to when I started at the department. We'd have known if there were any ultra-clever alternative means to develop mining blockchains."

Grace turned towards Daniel. "Explain about the safeguards hierarchy."

Daniel continued," You'll probably know most of this, but there's a sort of pecking order to the way we view the security safeguards around CNI that's the Critical National Infrastructure."

"For digital, as in the physical world, it is simply not possible to safeguard everything in the cyber world to the highest degree. Security resources are costly and limited, and therefore priority must be given to protecting the most important targets and those where an attack would cause the most damage."

"Ah yes," Rosie said, "The CNI priorities list. Energy, Comms and Finance"

Daniel continued, "For example, I think everyone agrees that nuclear power plants should receive excellent protection from physical attack. By contrast, it is simply not possible to provide that same level of security for every electrical substation — much less every transmission tower and power pole — on the lines between the nuclear plant and the consumers who receive the electricity. "

"By necessity, there is an array of "soft targets" somewhere in the electrical system, and indeed, our society is filled with vulnerable targets. "

"Targeting the smaller substations and so on is disruptive but not so effective, more an annoyance," said Rosie.

"Yes, Rosie, these soft targets are often chosen simply because of their vulnerability to terrorist attacks, especially by terrorist operatives who lack sophisticated tradecraft."

"Communications is another high priority area, and so are Financial Services. All three of Energy, Communications and Financial Services get high levels of support and protection."

Daniel continued: "However, there are still soft, vulnerable targets for each of these in the cyber realm. Some of them can and will be attacked in a manner that could result in death and destruction, though on a much smaller scale than a cyber warfare attack by a nation-state.

"In many ways, this would be similar to attempts by terrorists to obtain and use chemical or biological weapons and the difficulty they have faced in making these programs as effective as a nation state's chemical or biological weapons program."

At its simplest, someone can steal the copper from a train line between Cheltenham and Birmingham and create havoc because there's no communication or signalling. Sure, it disrupts many people, but it's not the same a stealing the entire signalling capability of Network Rail."

"Most terrorists consider that all they need is the cyber equivalent of a primitive chemical weapon or a pressure cooker bomb. As we progressively automate and interconnect our lives, we can see an increasing number of items attached to the Internet that a creative person could use to cause mayhem."

"The effect of their actions in this smaller way can still be disastrous and scary, which most of the terrorists would regard as 'job done'."

"Frankly, and I hope Grace won't mind me saying this, that's what the majority of the GCHQ effort is expended on intercepting. The smaller incidents that create chatter and can be headed off before they occur."

"It's also easier for us when we know where these people

prefer to communicate. Shutting down their broadcast bulletin boards sounds like a good thing but makes our life harder because we then have to find the next place or system that they are using to spread their messages."

"The cyber-fraud we are considering here is a whole different dimension. It's completely silent, systematised on a global scale and has the backing provided by a powerful nation-state."

"For the most part, the Internet does not stop at national borders, and it is quite common for hacks to be conducted from another country and for hackers to skip across the globe using compromised systems in several different countries to hide their trail."

Rosie added, "It means that cyberterrorists can hack transnationally without having to travel to the country where their target is located. The ultimate working from home."

"It's a whole extra level if the nation-state is directly sponsoring the offshore locations used as part of the hack," said Grace.

Daniel added, "But I suppose another consideration would be the possibility of an insider threat. As we've seen in cases like those involving Chelsea Manning and Edward Snowden, an insider can compromise a great deal of information. That would work for a routine cyber hack, like information stealing, but for something like this where the whole fundamental nature of the system is built to protect against hacks, then an insider would have limited use."

"There's also still the attack cycle used for the cyber currency," said Tyler

"There has to be a way to first inject the fake money into the system. Ironically, by the time the money has been presented to a bank, it already looks completely genuine. It follows all of the characteristics of cybercash, is properly tokenised and has the blockchain structure that everyone expects. That's what makes the plan so elegant."

"It implies that the system is kept away from prying eyes until the blockchain credibility has been established," said Tyler.

"And that's what we need to work against," said Daniel. "We need to think of the blockchain creation process as open to interception. If we can get to that stage, then we should be on to something."

"Yes, we need to create a kill chain of our own," said Daniel." We must find the places along their creation cycle where their efforts are vulnerable to detection — and also assume that they are on-guard for such probes."

Hi y'all

Bernard Driscoll had enough of the current situation. He knew that he'd now messed up two interviews, but it wasn't his fault.

The briefings he had been given were lousy.

There had been too little progress from his teams.

Their own findings meant his explanations sounded weak.

He would need to do something positive that showed global leadership.

Now he'd got a meeting with the Prime Minister. This wasn't likely to be a congratulatory meeting. He'd need something up his sleeve.

Unfortunately, he didn't have a perfect story at the moment. His own people were, for whatever reason, not behaving the way he had demanded.

He was at the point where he thought he would need external help to tip the scales back towards his own position.

The last thing he wanted was even more fragmentation from small teams. He was sure that the reason he was in the current mess was because he'd let the diverse units start to assert themselves.

Instead, it would be a lot better for him if he could take back control to SI6 and GCHQ. Then he would have a couple of units which he could control and could divert all of the funding back to these two leading players.

He decided that instead of involving yet another small private company to help him, it would be better to go to someone big and influential.

On this occasion, he could use the Americans.

There was hardly any downside. It would show Bernard Driscoll to be influential, powerful and decisive and yet ready to deploy a dramatically improved team to resolve the current situation.

He knew that this would make Amanda livid, but he would be making contact with Mary-Anne Piper from the American embassy.

Driscoll knew Mary-Anne would have a team in place somewhere in central London that could help him regain his balance on all of this. He needed to work out what he considered to be the loose cannons and the best way was to have some additional tricks up his sleeve.

He was on his way to see the PM when he called Mary-Anne, from the back of his car.

"Hello Mary-Anne, How's my favourite Texan? It's Bernard Driscoll, I need to talk to you."

"Hi Bern-hard," she said - she always pronounced it as two words and Bernard had become used to it.

"I guess this is about y'all bombs?" she said, "We've already called your controller about this to offer assistance but were told to run along."

"Yes," said Bernard, "It is about the bombs, but what I'm really looking for is some kind of support from you. Maybe some help from Langley too?"

"This is, indeed, unusual, What, then, don't ya have?"

"I'm concerned that things may have a certain 'momentum', answered Driscoll.

"Are you asking us to support you? How unusual here in London."

"I know," said Bernard, "but I'm concerned that things are running away from themselves at the moment. I need some background help to ensure that we regain equilibrium on all of this."

Mary-Anne paused, and Bernard wondered if she was thinking about his television interviews.

He knew that he was in a slightly awkward situation with all of this. The way the television had wrongly portrayed him made him look like a bit of a buffoon.

He would need to keep himself polite when talking to Mary-Anne - he needed her cooperation because otherwise he would be forced to use some of the subcontractors.

"Okay," Mary-Anne said, "I think we can support y'all. We have a team based in central London who are pretty good at these bomb situations."

"I assume that's what you need?" she asked.

"Not exactly," said Barnard, "It's a bit more complicated than that. How about we meet somewhere, and I explain what is happening?"

"Why don't you come on over to one of our places?" said Mary-

Anne, "We still have that small station just off of Grosvenor Square near to where the main embassy used to be."

. . .

The side of Grosvenor Square looked like many of the other tall townhouses in that part of London. It wasn't inside any of the recognisable embassy buildings, and this has meant that people like Bernard could get into the building quite quickly compared with access through embassy doors and security routes.

Ironically this secure building was more accessible for those people in the know than the main embassy, which was now situated in a huge sugar cube of a building in South London.

"I see you still have a regular space set up here," said Bernard as he greeted Mary-Anne.

It looked more like a management consultancy with a smart hotel-like reception area, a few non-descript wall posters and nothing displayed in the typical US government typefaces.

"We've tried to make ourselves look inconspicuous on the outside here," said Mary-Anne," Of course we have a few more specialised facilities around the back."

"Yes, I feel as if I could book my next holiday here," said Driscoll," Look, I require help, across at GCHQ. Linking your NSA with our intel should speed things up. I want to catch those bombers, fast."

"Okay, but you'll owe me, the next time I need a small favour."

"Your favours are never small," replied Driscoll realising what he said and that it was he who was in deep trouble, with Mary-Anne as his source of rescue.

"We've found one of them," said Mary-Anne, "At least we found the woman who was sent to do the tidying up."

"The Russians even sent a substitute to be caught, a genuine low-level office secretary."

Driscoll looked interested, "Who have you got?"

"It's someone we've been tracking for quite a while. Alya Sokolov did some nasty stuff in Washington, but then flew over to Paris and then London. We've been watching her all along."

"Her name is Alya Sokolov, as well as a few aliases. She's a Russian fixer, for the FSB. Highly trained and quite difficult to catch in the middle of anything."

"Wait, so have you detained her?" asked Driscoll.

"We might have asked her to step into a black van," said Mary-Anne.

"And?"

"She's good, very good, but right now we think she's trying to bargain her way out of the situation. We pulled her after the bombing, when she was ferrying a couple of the bomb drivers around London. She'd got traces of Semtex on her clothes. Careless, really. And highly unusual."

"Okay," said Driscoll, "Then I take it you are in and will provide assistance. It saves us getting all messy about the US government extracting Russians from the streets of London."

Mary-Anne does Cheltenham

Amanda Miller's phone rang.

It was Mary-Anne from the American Embassy.

"Hello, Mary-Anne, and to what do I owe this unexpected call?"

"Bern-hard Driscoll, actually," Amanda could almost feel the smirk on Mary-Anne's face.

"Ah, yes, Bernard. Sorry to say he hasn't mentioned anything."

"We've been asked to give you some assistance," replied Mary-Anne.

Amanda looked aghast but kept her voice level.

"I guess this must be a new request. I thought we were already keeping you fairly well in the loop?"

"That's right," said Mary-Anne, "Although right now I think it is us that need to keep you in the loop. We've been asked to come along to your operations room. Bern-hard was most insistent."

Amanda was standing outside of her own operations room.

Now, because of Driscoll, she'd need to set up another room that could be used safely by the Americans as well as her own people.

It would potentially dilute what they were doing unless she decided to give the Americans unfettered access to their information and controls.

"I guess we can work together on this," she smiled into the phone.

"That's great because I'm already on the way down to Cheltenham," replied Mary-Anne. We're on the outskirts of London now."

Amanda was furious with Driscoll. Not only had he arranged this with Mary-Anne, but he'd not had the courtesy to advise Amanda of what he'd agreed. She'd have to cross-check it all with him now before Mary-Anne arrived. Amanda asked Grace for help to pick another secure location in Cheltenham for Mary-Anne's visit. Grace identified Fiddler's Green, a small stately home generally used for training purposes, although it was heavily wired to the main GCHQ location.

Amanda considered that she could isolate GCHQ from the prying eyes of the Americans and their propensity to drop little bugs and wiretaps all over the place.

Tyler and Rosie were unphased by another move of location. They had been in so many buildings that another one didn't seem to be anything special.

"Cool drive, though," said Rosie to Tyler as they looked out of the front windows towards the greenery and sweeping drive of the location.

"Yes," said Tyler, "It feels as if we've somehow arrived, like in a James Bond movie."

"Or Brideshead Revisited."

"That one was straight."

"Straight? Brideshead?"

"You know what I mean. The drive for Brideshead was straight."

There was a commotion at the front gate. It swung inwards, and a large black SUV entered, headlights on. Then a second one, then a black American saloon car, then a black armoured security van, then a black truck and another two SUVs.

"Subtle, or what?" asked Rosie. They both laughed.

The convoy swung around the drive and pulled up at the main entrance.

Amanda was already standing by the front door. Several suited Americans stepped from the leading and second SUV.

Mary-Anne emerged from the black car, smiling.

"Wow, that's quite an entrance!" said Amanda, "Welcome to Downton Abbey."

"Well, we are transporting special cargo," replied Mary Anne.

Amanda looked confused. Driscoll had not mentioned anything when she spoke to him to cross-check that this had all been agreed.

"We've brought Alya Sokolov, I thought you'd like that!" said Mary-Anne.

"Thank you for coming along," Amanda lied.

"We are pleased to help. We've brought one of our standard computer and comms packages to get started quickly. The teams are bomb and terrorism specialists. We've also brought along some computer specialists because we understand that there may be another dimension to this?"

Amanda had to play that she didn't know about this aspect. Mary-Anne might have been fishing for information.

"We are mainly focused on the bomb threat causes at the moment. As the minister said – the bombs were both placed at our own buildings. We've had several people own up to them, but none of them looks like a credible source — pranksters and lunatics rather than extremists.

"Do you have any reason to think that this is state-sponsored?" asked Mary-Anne.

"We are not ruling it out," said Amanda.

"Look, I get it that you've put us in a bubble here," said Mary-Anne, "To be honest I was expecting to see Grace Fielding. I suppose I'd do the same when an ally comes to the NSA; quietly drop them into a suburb of Washington."

"The United States is keen to assist with this search," continued Mary-Anne, "To avoid any potential embarrassment down the way. We've already questioned Alya, and we know about the two bombers and their escape routes. We think Alya has been cornered and wants a way out."

Amanda noticed that Mary-Anne did not mention the computer hacks and wondered if this was still unknown to the Americans. A simple bombing might be a more reasonable motive.

"What's your backstory on Alya Sokolov?" asked Amanda.

"Same as yours, probably, a major disruptor in the States. Fixer from a number of Russian missions which need to be tidied away. It was her unlucky break that we were already tracking her when she decided to assist here in London. We'd been following her for a couple of months."

Mary-Anne looked straight at Amanda, "So let me try making a couple of guesses. Bernard Driscoll hasn't said any of this, so I'm running on my own theory here, not from some supplied source."

Mary Ann continued, "Suppose one of your teams had discovered something? Maybe something that was compromising to a government. Heck – perhaps even to the Americans. In our way of working, we'd have to push it out into the open. I don't think we'd use the blunt instruments of bombs, but we'd undoubtedly run something on the diplomatic channels to get it into the open. I'm guessing that most of the NATO countries would do the same. "

"Look – check if you want – with Driscoll or bypass him – if you can – to try to find out if we've been up to something. The short answer is that – to my knowledge - we haven't."

"But if I'm right then, another county or nation-state might be trying something more basic to push the information, or your discovery or whatever it is out into the open. They might want it to be visible, or more likely they want to shut it down."

"The next source we would consider would be one of the usual suspects like ISIS or some other variation on a middle eastern terrorist organisation. The style doesn't quite fit, though. They'd not use such small devices, and they'd plant them where there would be more of a blast pattern and probably kill a whole bunch of civilians in the process."

"This looks to be far more surgical than that. And by the way, I can't see ISIS missing a trick to claim the bombing for themselves. It's not their style."

"You also have a history with the Irish Republicans spanning back into the last century. They always have a protocol for their bombs, calls, warning, reasons explained. And we are pretty good at intercepting them as well. Nothing like that."

"It suggests that this has been done by someone as part of a more complex process. A lone operator? Hardly. There are too many moving parts. Organised crime? Where's the demand? What do they want?"

"I'm not completely discounting lunatics, but they would still need funding, and almost always they would be putting up demands. A video on YouTube, for example. But so far there's nothing. It's like a closed system. Except for the silent Russian connection."

"Your thinking so far is close to ours," said Amanda. She was impressed that the Americans had been able to work this through without access to her information.

"It makes us think that this is more of a private matter," continued Mary-Anne, "Something within the security community. A message from them – whoever they are - to you. Along the lines of back off – don't continue with whatever it is you've been doing."

Amanda remained quiet at this point. This was where Mary-Anne's and her view of things started to differ. The Americans didn't seem to know about Marcus's disappearance from the Hammersmith hotel.

"I'm guessing that there is something that you have that others either want or want to stop?" asked Mary-Anne.

"This is the core of the way that we can move this forward and that I can potentially help you, "she continued, "and don't forget, I bring the gift of a Russian operative to you."

Amanda was thinking quickly. She would need something for the Americans, to try to enlist their support without giving away more than was necessary. Amanda decided to play for a small amount of time. She would release the information about Marcus and the paper, but only after his document had been modified.

"Look," she said.," You've got a pretty good grasp of this. I'm genuinely impressed with how much you've deduced. We've got some more to give you, but I suggest we run a team briefing to you and your whole team at 6 pm. That will give me a chance to put together the relevant documents and pictures.

Amanda knew that she'd need to work on a sanitised version of Marcus's paper. Keep in the rouble manipulation but lose the references to cybercash. She would need to read the redacted version herself, although she also needed the version for the Americans to look as if it was the whole paper and not an edit.

Mary-Anne nodded to Amanda.

"Look I get it that you don't really want us here. I get it that you've been driven into this by your charming boss. I understand that he didn't tell you he was doing this and that it was my phone call that was the first you had heard. We still need to work together, though. I think this is a time when you can use our help."

Amada nodded and smiled back to Mary-Anne,

"Go on - tell me your nickname for Bernard," she asked.

"It's Huffer," said Mary-Anne.

They both laughed.

Amanda thought she would need to play this carefully, but she could see that the Americans could potentially be very useful. She decided that she quite liked Mary-Anne.

Sanitised

An hour later, Amanda was in the middle of the now-filled control room at the offsite facility.

There was a whole new bank of technology already running, based on the systems that the Americans had brought along. It looked as if they had decided to bring as many shiny toys to create the most impressive picture possible.

Amanda had the newly printed and individually numbered briefing packs which covered the additional development around Marcus. This was potentially new information for the Americans.

Amanda made sure it removed any references to cyber currency and did not include any of the information that Marcus had mooted around America's involvement in reducing the value of the rouble through economic warfare.

Amanda thought this was a good compromise. It supported the theories of the Americans and moved things along enough to mean that they would have something to get their teeth into. It was also a quick way to shake the tree to see whether the Americans had any additional information to divulge.

Amanda ran the briefing. She added the disappearance of

Marcus and Marcus's paper. She could see it was enough.

Her own substitute team and the Americans were learning this new level of information together. Now it would be interesting to see whether the Americans could unearth anything new.

Tyler and Rosie looked on - this was a far cry from the office of three that they had shared with Marcus.

"It's as if the American style of hustle management has crossed over into her own team's way of working," said Rosie.

"Yes," agreed Tyler, he knew in his heart of hearts that the team deployed in this group from their own departments were not the sharpest knives in the box. More likely, they were the people who could be most easily released at short notice to form a scratch team.

Grace was informed of Alya Sokolov's presence in the offsite facility. She owed one to Mary-Anne for this uncanny piece of tracking.

"I'll be visiting OS12," she said, I'd like to bring an interrogation team."

She dialled for a car and made her way to the front entrance of the complex. Several other members of her team had gathered. She noticed it included one of the on-site lawyers.

"Okay, we're going to meet a Russian agent. She will want to cut a deal," she explained.

A small bus arrived. Everyone climbed aboard.

Tyler was watching when the bus arrived at the entrance to the driveway.

"I think this will be one of ours," he said, "A small bus, not a whole convoy of late-model SUVs."

Rosie smiled back. There had to be some humour in it all.

They could see the team disembark and start to move through the building. Rosie and Tyler knew they were heading for The Pen. The name given to the detention suite.

Rosie and Tyler made their way upstairs to a small viewing room and selected the right monitor channel to watch proceedings.

"Hello Alya," started one of the interrogators.

"You know what I've asked for," she replied, "You provide me with the funds and the new identity, and I'll turn over to you. If my previous employer knows about this, he will have to disown me in any case."

"Disown you, or worse," said the interrogator.

"We need other information from you first. The reason for the bombs."

"You know how it works. I know my mission. This time it's three Extractions. The other operatives know their missions, but we don't get told the big picture. I can't help. Look you've got me; you know I'm burned. I'm not just bargaining with you. That's all I know. In any case, the two drivers were cutouts. Not even Russian. One of them didn't even speak Russian."

"Two extractions, the drivers. Tell us about the third extraction?"

"That was the C-SOC operative. Marcus Barton. The man from the hotel in West London. See, I am co-operating."

"Okay, so what happened to Marcus Barton? "

"I was asked to do this after I arrived in the UK. The two bomber extractions were requested when I was still in France.

It was from the same handler though, Alexander Pakshenko. I genuinely thought he was Russian, but now I think he was a double working for the Americans."

"Taking Marcus was easy. Hotel cleaners, Dart gun. Four to move him out on a trolley. Elevator to ground and then into a laundry van. I was asked to keep him as a bargaining chip, so he is in a safe house. Now, I want you to find him, as a little piece of grit for the people who misled me."

"Thank God, Marcus is still around. So, where is he?" asked Rosie.

"You'll have to ask Mary-Anne Piper, the Americans have him," replied Alya.

"There's still something about this that doesn't add up," said Tyler.

"Rosie, I want to retake a look at those videos, especially for the first bomb. To check if there could be anyone else involved," Tyler requested.

He was thinking back to the walk he'd done along to the first scene of mayhem. The Americans flourish of arrival had reminded him of something.

We've got the videos in Comms 12, said Rosie, "Although, I don't have a clue where that room is."

"I think its downstairs in the basement," answered Tyler as they set off.

Video

Tyler and Rosie were in the video suite, about to watch the first bombing.

The video showed a small clock at the start, which showed real-time feeds from the event. Tyler noticed it started a good 5 minutes earlier than the Press and Media coverage videos that he'd seen previously. From the time just after he'd bought his lunch.

They were told that the editing together of several separate streams had provided the best closeups of the unfolding scene, but that they could get to the originals based upon timestamps as the video played.

It started. Busy traffic. The van pulling into the kerbside. Double yellow lines. The driver climbed out. Pedestrians and people walking around. A lone figure walks down the steps from the secure building. This time Tyler recognises it as Matt. A large SUV appears, which looks similar to the ones the Americans have just driven up the drive to OS12. A large sliding door opens. A single figure is hauled inside.

A sudden explosion, most of the blast goes upwards. Dust. Pedestrians on the ground. Traffic stopped and some cars attempting to get around obstructions in the road.

"That's Matt," said Tyler, "I'm sure that is Matt. The part of the video had been cut off from the earlier ones I've seen."

The black van drives slowly away.

A taxi appears, and the van driver climbs in. Blue lights.

"I remember it," said Tyler, "Damn, I remember seeing that black van. But I was trying to make sense of the bigger picture at the time. I thought that van was part of the first responders."

"So, Matt has been hauled away by someone? And yet the story is that he was killed?"

"I don't know, I don't understand," said Tyler.

"This changes everything," said Tyler.

"Matt is still out there. When we looked at the memory stick, we found transactions to a company called Gun Street Holdings, which if ever there was a Matt named company, then that would be it."

"Huh?" asked Rosie.

"Gun Street Girls - a track by Tom Waits - Matt was mad about Tom Waits."

"Now it looks as if someone lifted him, even ahead of the blast. There was a story put about that he'd been killed, but I think he's out there somewhere."

"How about we find the banking details for Gun Street? "Asked Rosie.

"Good idea," said Tyler,

"This should be an easier search, especially through GCHQ."

Sure enough, an address came up. Chelsea Bridge Wharf, SW8,

west London, close to the river. Tyler didn't recognise it.

"Okay, I'm going to take a look," he said.

"I'm coming with you," said Rosie.

They called for a vehicle to take them back to London.

London Apartment

In London, they arrived at an expensive-looking apartment building on the South Bank. The address of Gun Street Holdings. Nothing was shown on the map, and all they had was an apartment block number.

The general impression was of quiet, well-heeled metro living.

"I think we should go to the actual apartment," said Tyler. "Matt knows me, but he also won't have an escape route if we do that."

They had to loiter around the entrance to the block. There was a double entrance key fob system, and they had to tailgate in past two separate locked gates to get to the elevator.

Tyler pressed the 8th floor. He hoped that the reverse entry address lookup system from the bank account that GCHQ used would be accurate.

They stood outside the door.

Tyler pressed the bell and heard its cheery ding inside.

A clank of metal and the door was opened.

"Matt!" said Tyler.

"Tyler, what on earth! - How did you find me!"

"I think I could ask you very similar questions," said Tyler.

"You'd better come in," said Matt.

"I'm glad to see you, but know you are both in danger being here," said Matt.

"Hello, by the way, my name is Matt Stevens, I'm a friend of Tyler's."

"I feel as if I know you already," said Rosie.

Tyler looked around. Sleek kitchen, floor to ceiling glass windows, a view across the River Thames. Fancy modern furniture.

"Beer?" asked Matt.

"Sure," said Rosie, Tyler nodded.

"Okay, Explanations?" Asked Tyler

"I needed to disappear," said Matt, "I was under intense pressure."

He stepped over to Tyler and hugged him, slapping him on the back.

"Hey, man, it's good to see you!"

He flipped the two beers open.

"Glasses, frosted and cool?" he asked.

"You bet," smiled Tyler. Rosie nodded.

"Pressure. From whom? Who was putting you under pressure?

"Asked Tyler

"The Russians," said Matt,

Rosie and Tyler nodded.

"It was mixed up with the cyber currency," explained Matt. He poured the beers carefully a quarter into the glass.

"The system became too much of a good thing. It wasn't just the British that spotted what we were doing. I know they gave us both a job on the strength of it," He looked to Tyler and handed him the glass and the bottle.

"But later on, I worked out how to build a closed blockchain, which the Russians then started to use."

"It was economic engineering, via the Russian state - I assume you worked that out. Because the blockchains were in their own self-contained system, it was very difficult to prove that they were fraudulent after a critical mass of them had been created. You know what, I think Kyle had predicted that when we were all together at the flat."

Matt continued, sipping on his beer.

"I could see it was going to bring down economies, and I started to get worried. The Russians are very susceptible to rake-offs, and everybody must get paid. Although I was getting a tidy commission, I was also the one to blame if it was discovered."

"That's when the Americans approached me. I know, British, Russian, Americans. Nothing like being popular."

"The Americans came along. They wanted to stop the system. They could see Russia was using it as a weapon. They never admitted that they had started the whole thing with a much more basic model of their own."

"But you knew the Americans had been using a similar technique to sanction Russia?" asked Rosie.

"Oh yes, although I chose to keep quiet about my copious proof of the USA sabotaging the Russian economy. I thought it would get me into even deeper water," answered Matt.

He continued, "The Americans said they had proof that I had engineered the cyber coin system and that it was being used to provide Russia with material advantages in world financial circles. You know the hacker world is fairly small, so I made some enquiries to find out who had been checking up on me. It turned out to be a low-grade hacker, who was quite lucky and intercepted some of my traffic. He'd never have been able to work out the math involved in blockchain optimisation."

Tyler nodded, he knew Matt and Kyle were the propeller heads compared to him while they all lived together in the Kensington flat. Only in the outside world had he discovered just how simplistic the use of maths was, largely thanks to the rise of Excel.

"The Americans made me a deal. They could see I wanted to get out from under the Russians. Talk about Cold War. This shows just how quietly powerful cyber is in influence politics. Forget about tipping elections, with this stuff you could tip whole economies."

"The Americans said they could make me disappear - if you know what I mean - as long as I source them some code to stop the cyber process and potentially wind it back. They said I could keep my gains and that they would rehouse me and assist with an identity change."

"What's not to like?" I thought, "Until they started using bombs as a cover for my extraction."

"What?" asked Rosie, "You're saying the bombs were a cover?"

"Yes, although I didn't know that at the time." My handler,

Aron Baynes, explained that they would need two explosions. The real one and a second one to throw people off the trail from the first one."

"Well that certainly worked, now we've got all manner of terrorist plot theories circulating and no-one plausible owning up to the bombs," said Tyler.

"They persuaded me that an accident would be the simplest way to extract me, and then I could rebuild my life without the threat of being followed. I'll admit it, I was scared in case they were really going to blow me up. I had to resort to some insurance of my own. I told them I'd already set up an If_I_die.org message which would prove very inconvenient if I were to completely disappear.

"I may just still need it now that you guys have found me. Well done, Tyler"

"Oh, and forgive me, Cheers," He clinked the three beer glasses together.

Rosie chipped in, "Not forgetting that we found you by harnessing the entire power of GCHQ, SI6 and the FBI."

"No, I agree, but there's equivalent power in the Russian mob. Take a look downstairs at this apartment block. It even has a Russian concierge."

"You know something?" said Tyler, "You are pretty central to what happens next back in Cheltenham."

"I think so, said Matt, "But I'm also well-hidden at the moment."

"Have you ever ridden in a helicopter?" asked Rosie.

"Because I think this is the ideal time, and we are close to the Battersea heliport too."

"Can you do that?" asked Tyler.

"I think I can do just about anything with the knowledge we have, " answered Rosie.

"From here to the terminal is only about 10 minutes by taxi," said Matt, "Although it is a bit of a zig-zag route."

"Ideal," said Rosie," that'll confuse anyone following."

"Do I need to pack anything?" asked Matt,

"Just your 'Go Bag'," said Tyler, referring to the overnight bags they used to keep at the ready back in their flat dwelling days.

"Okay," said Matt. "When we get outside, there's a cab rank opposite, by the hotel."

Tyler and Rosie nodded. They had seen the hotel on their way into the apartment block.

"Let's get flying!" said Tyler.

"So...How long will it take?" asked Matt.

"To Fiddler's Green...About 45 minutes," answered Rosie.

Creative

The helicopter landed directly in the grounds of the stately home.

Matt, Rosie and Tyler climbed out.

Grace was standing on the apron with crossed arms.

"Welcome to Fiddler's Green and OS12, and you must be the extremely elusive Matt?" asked Grace.

"That's right, Tyler and I go back a long way."

"So I've heard, and I gather you know about cybercash too?"

"That's right, I've been fairly successful."

"Let's go inside, I have a few questions for you, Matt."

They sat in a large room, with a central table. It reminded Tyler of a boardroom for an old-fashioned company. It was officially known as The Drawing Room.

Grace, Amanda, Rosie, Tyler, and Daniel sat around the table. Rosie had told Matt to wait in a separate room.

There was a silver tray containing a thermal coffee pot, some white mugs and some small packets of biscuits at one end of the table.

"So Alya didn't know why she was running extraction on the two drivers?" questioned Rosie.

"Or exactly who asked her to do it," added Tyler.

"Could it be that the Americans somehow duped Alya into the mission?"

"We have an interesting question for Mary-Anne."

Grace was eating a chicken wrap. Rosie assumed that it had continued to be a non-stop activity for Grace in the Ops Room.

Grace asked, "So how, exactly, can I help you?"

"We think we've uncovered something quite unusual," said Rosie," We think Alya might have been receiving instructions from the Americans - but without realising it.

"She's asked for British protection and asylum now and is prepared to be a witness to what is happening. Something doesn't gel though. She says she was tasked with coming to the UK to perform an extraction job for the two van drivers who drove the bombs. The thing is, she met them both and doesn't think either of them was Russian. She described them as cutouts.

"That's quite normal, though," answered Grace, nibbling the last part of the wrap.

"Russian agents will often get last-minute unsuspecting people to drive or do parts of their dirty work."

"We think that the vans were sponsored by another country, that's all," said Rosie.

"We've robust evidence that points to the vans being run by the

USA."

"If that is the case, then it is an extreme allegation," said Grace.

"It would imply that the US was running a mini terrorist threat on the streets of London."

"Yes, the stakes would have to be high for that to be the case," answered Rosie.

"Have you any proof?" Asked Grace.

"We do, we think that one of the originators of the cyber fraud was Matt, a colleague of Tyler's. He had been hired by our own security forces and had been working out of the first bombed building."

"He's the one reported casualty from the first blast."

"I remember," said Grace.

"Yes, but we've just found him, very much alive and kicking, over in west London. He claims that he had done a deal with the Americans to re-house him under a new identity.

"Why?" Asked Grace, "Why would the Americans do that?"

"Well, Matt was one of the designers of the cyber currency machine. He did it with Tyler here when they lived together in a flat."

"It was a student project to raise some cash," explained Tyler, "It was just a bit more successful than we imagined. It's how Matt and I got to be working here. You, well the Department, offered us both jobs."

Grace nodded, "Okay, but I can't see why that would bring in the Americans?"

"That's where the full version of the Marcus paper comes in.

Marcus had identified that there was some manipulation of markets occurring because the Russians seemed to have a magic money tree.

"It turns out that there was an original plan exploited by the US government to manipulate Russian currency and then Russia discovered it and decided to play a similar game but using some redeveloped crypto software.

"That was the tweaked software that Matt introduced, except it was too successful, Matt himself got cold feet, and then the Americans rounded him up to threaten him. Unless he helped the US, he'd pay the consequence, but if he helped them, then America would help him get a new identity.

"So, he accepted the American offer. The Americans offered to make him disappear.

"In return for what?" asked Grace.

"Yes, you've got it. The US wanted him to roll back the crypto software. Ideally, to anonymously discredit it. Ideally, to reduce the value of the cybercash created for Russia, too.

"Now, the strange part. The Americans wanted two bombs so that they could run interference. They used hired help to drive the van, but through a double agent Pakashenko they apparently asked Alya to provide the extraction of the drivers. Alya was fooled and ran an altogether a professional operation. But Alya noticed a departure from tradecraft. The drivers were not Russian, nor, I gather, from any of the normal Russian sources. She thought the mission was too high stakes to have been run by outsiders.

Grace nodded, "Do you remember what Mary-Anne said in that early briefing. That the Americans had been following Alya for a couple of months? Is it possible that they set a trap to catch her in London? She did seem to drop into their laps somewhat?"

"Yes. That could be, although it is going to be tricky to get Mary-Anne to admit anything, assuming she even knows?"

Grace nodded, "She will know. She's the top US controller in London. I might have an idea," she said.

"Here's my thinking," said Grace, "We've access to plenty of hot material here, in GCHQ."

"We need to take Mary-Anne to a room where some of it is being processed, something she will know about and then we can - how can I put this - creatively augment the material with something that will be a source of embarrassment."

"Can it be directly related to the Alya situation?" Asked Amanda.

"Ideally, yes," said Grace. "It should show that we know that the USA has been looking for a lure to get Alya into the UK."

"We might have to wing it, but somehow we can confront Mary-Anne with the information, to find out what she knows."

"Alya has told us most of the information anyway, but it will be useful to see whether Mary-Anne knows about the deep cyber money plot?"

"So, what's the underlying material going to be?" asked Rosie.

"I think we can use 'The Panama Papers'," said Grace." There's so much of it that Mary-Anne would only know about it selectively in any case."

Rosie began, "Tyler, the Panama Papers were an unprecedented leak of 11.5 million files from the database of the world's fourth biggest offshore law firm, Mossack Fonseca. Everyone in the intelligence community knew about the leak, although few could keep track of the detail."

Tyler nodded," I remember something about them, I think

there was a movie or something."

"Yes, originally, the records were obtained from an anonymous source by the Süddeutsche Zeitung, which shared them with the International Consortium of Investigative Journalists. The ICIJ then shared them with a large network of international partners, including the Guardian and the BBC, who began analysing what was in the files."

"I remember, wasn't David Cameron's father involved in some way?" said Tyler.

"Yes, he was, as was a friend of Putin and more than 100 politicians, all using offshore tax havens."

"But no cybercash connection?"

"No, that's right, just not-so-simple tax evasion."

"The documents showed the myriad ways in which the rich can exploit secretive offshore tax regimes.

"It included a $2bn trail leading all the way to Vladimir Putin. The Russian president's best friend is at the centre of a scheme in which money from Russian state banks is hidden offshore."

"So how will we use this information with Mary-Anne?"

"We'll have to be a little creative," answered Grace.

PART THREE

Enrollment

"She smiled at him
like they were about to rob a bank together."

— *Rachel Kushner, The Flamethrowers*

National Security

Matt, Daniel, Rosie and Tyler were in a planning session in the main operations room.

Matt spoke to Daniel, "We have to find a way into the Russian system so we can proliferate the new code to all of their nodes."

"This is like a classic virus problem," said Daniel.

"Surely you guys at GCHQ have plenty of people that are well versed in the ways of viruses?", asked Matt.

"Yes, although we are usually on the receiving end of the virus rather than the people that are creating it," answered Daniel.

"Some companies out there are specialists in this kind of thing", said Tyler.

"Sure, nowadays they even advertise overtly on the internet. Some price-lists show the value of the type of exploits that they create," answered Matt.

"I know," said Daniel, "but they are usually the bad people we are trying to stop."

"Well, obviously, we need to get one of them onto our payroll," said Rosie.

"Tricky, if it ever got out that GCHQ and SI6 were hiring overt bad-guy hackers," said Daniel.

"Duh, don't you think the public already suspect that?" asked Rosie, "But first, we need a cover, but one that doesn't just spring up. It needs to have a lengthy heritage."

"Okay, how about a security consultancy with about three years track record, fixing corporate firewalls and the like?" asked Tyler.

"You mean Kyle?" asked Rosie.

"Yes, he said he'd hope we would hire him one day. This could be it - I've already cleared it with Amanda, and she's sent a car," smiled Tyler.

"This is crazy," said Matt, "The Hereford Square gang is finally back together. All we need is a sourdough pizza."

"From Franco Manca on the Brompton Road," said Tyler.

And, as if on cue, the control room door opened and in strode sunglassed Kyle, complete with a backpack.

"Hey guys, that was pretty cool, having a car come to pick me up to drive me to the middle of nowhere. If you hadn't called me up first, I'd have thought this was some pretty elaborate hoax."

Matt and Tyler smiled and slapped Kyle on the back.

"Man, we have some shizzle to tell you," said Matt.

"These are Rosie and Daniel, our partners in crime," said Tyler.

"Crime," said Kyle, "I don't like the sound of that. I've just got back from Tel Aviv, and I was given such a hard time getting out of the country. Forgive me if I sound jaded, but they didn't seem to believe a word of what I said. Mind you, I suppose I was coming back from a security conference. I should have said I'd been on holiday or something."

"Right, Kyle, you said you'd liked to work for us, here's your proper opportunity. And what we really need right now is your company," asked Tyler.

"Yes, you mentioned that on the phone, but I'm not sure that I understand."

"We want you to be a well-established security storefront. Commissioning some specialist hackers for a new project."

"Oh yes, is this lawful?" asked Kyle.

"Let's say it is the interests of National Security, "answered Rosie.

"Hmm. Go on then," said Kyle.

"We want you to recruit a team of virus writers," said Tyler, "Using one of the Warez packs. We want it to be good enough to hack through Matt's cyber currency algorithm."

"What? Hack Matt? But he's here?"

"Exactly," said Matt, "We need it to look like a spirited and lucky attack, I want to destroy the blockchain that we've been creating and to discredit the algorithm."

"Won't that cause someone quite a bit of bother?" asked Kyle.

"Yes, exactly, but it must look anonymous."

"I see, but I suppose you'll provide a few hints and tips to help crack the algorithm?" asked Kyle.

"Yes, I'll provide them to you, and you will provide them to the hackers."

"It's like a form of sabotage," said Kyle.

"It is, we are unwinding what Matt has provided."

"May I ask why?" asked Kyle.

"Let's say some bad people have got hold of it," answered Rosie.

"But you are telling me that this is legitimate, above-board, legal?" asked Kyle.

"Not exactly, but it is On Her Majesty's Secret Service," answered Tyler.

"You can't get cooler than that, double-O-8?"

Matt had been preparing a wall chart.

He stepped back to take a look.

"It's incredible, he said," Nearly all of the hacks are theft related. No-one is interested in wrecking the algorithms. I thought I knew about this stuff, but it's when you get asked an awkward question that you realise that it's like a one-way valve.

"As cryptocurrencies have proliferated widely and as security systems designed to protect customers and exchanges have grown more sophisticated, hacks and instances of theft have also continued to take place.

"Even the biggest cryptocurrency exchange and the most significant players in the digital currency world are not necessarily safe.

"To be honest, that is good for our plan, because it means the people hacked won't be as surprised.

Matt continued, "I've taken a look at a few of the more prominent hacks - trying to link them together.

“First, there was Coinrail. A South Korean exchange was hacked, and thieves took about $37 million worth of digital currency, mainly in the form of tokens.

“Then a related smaller one. South Korea's Bithumb. That hack took $30 million in tokens. Although the exchange has promised that customers will see no impact on their wallets, Bithumb has not come out unscathed. Bithumb was formerly the sixth-largest exchange around the world based on trade volumes but has since dropped to 10th place. That attack focused on Bithumb's hot wallet. A pretty easy form of attack.

“BitCoin lost around 11% of its total value in the immediate aftermath of the hack, although it remains unclear to what degree the Coinrail hack had an impact on this fluctuation. The exchange was shut down in the wake of the attack.

“Then the Italians lost $195 Million when the Italian exchange BitGrail was hacked, and the nano token stolen.

“Another attack was on the Japanese exchange Coincheck, which cost it over 500 million coins valued at about $500 million.

"Wow," said Tyler, "half a billion dollars?"

Mattt continued, "Yes, and like Bithumb's hot wallet attack, this was an online real-time attack, and some say it was the most significant direct cybercrime ever committed. Amazingly the system survived and is still running.

“Then there’s the pyramid schemes. OneCoin was allegedly a Ponzi scheme with pyramid selling to boost the value of the coins. The Russian lady who fronted it did a runner.”

"I heard about that one," said Tyler, "The Russian Crypto Queen. It was all over the news. Something like $4 billion stolen."

"Yes, and it poses a problem for us. We'll be doing the biggest hack of all time, but it won't be as noticeable because of these other ones. It also tells me something of the method, which I think will be to manipulate the blockchains by infiltrating the hot wallets."

"Hot wallets?" asked Rosie, "What's that about?"

"A hot wallet is online," explained Kyle, "That's the vulnerability. If we can get to plenty of online hot wallets, we can make them malfunction and render the currency held invalid. It's like theft, but instead of taking the currency, we are destroying it in-situ. Burning the money while it is still in the wallet."

"It will take some explaining to whoever we hire to cover this!" exclaimed Kyle. "They will think we are mad."

"Or," said Tyler, "How about creating a parallel universe?" simply move the money from where it is stored to somewhere else, without having direct access to it?"

"That's not a bad idea," said Daniel, "We could move all the money to a new blockchain series, just one for which there is no known key. It would take millennia to crack it."

"Okay, but if that's what we do, then we tell the hackers that we have the key so that they think we are just regular thieves," said Kyle. "This is getting more bizarre by the minute."

"Welcome to the world of Crypto-jacking," said Daniel.

"I've just been to a security conference, and yet no-one even mentioned that as a thing," said Kyle.

"I think we can probably help your hired company," said

Daniel. "We have a few specialist items of our own."

Kyle and Daniel huddled together; they would prepare an advertisement for the internet, requesting specialised code and services to support their virus attack.

"We'll probably get back some bit kits," said Daniel. "They usually try to sell us some part-written code."

"I think I'll be able to sift through that," said Kyle, "We've run across many of the players."

Daniel clicked a button and the advertisement went live.

"You wait, he said, "The bots will find it first. Then the serious offers."

Sure enough, in minutes, the advert yielded several bids.

"That was almost instantaneous!" said Tyler.

"Yes, the hackers monitor the main auction sites and run automated responses very quickly if there is a request," answered Kyle.

"Let's take a look,"

He listed the bids on his screen, they varied from less than $100k to some that were into the low millions of dollars.

"The pricing has very little to do with the quality," said Kyle, "and the specs they provide are quite often also copied from one another. It's the Wild West out there, and everyone is hoping that someone will give actual money in advance."

"Here we are," said Kyle, "This one looks good, I know the company and the kits they are offering have some track record."

"I'd have to get my guys to insert the key recognition into the hacking kit. That will take some time, but it means there's a guaranteed result rather than a speculative payload."

"We then need to think of a few targets to aim it at,"

"So, we are sending a virus, preloaded with the key of the Russian cyber coin, into the wild?" asked Rosie.

"That's right, but we need to send it to a few other exchanges as well so that it doesn't look too specific. It is a bit like covering our tracks. A few from the top ten and maybe a French, Swiss and Chinese exchange."

"What about the Americans?"

"Good point, but if we leave them out, then it does start to suggest a certain origin for the product."

How long will it take to build this?" asked Grace.

"About a couple of days if we can get the kit and I can use my own people," said Kyle.

"That's fine, but please keep Daniel involved. I think he might be able to help you too."

"Agreed," said Kyle.

Driscoll loses it

Amanda's phone rang.

It was Driscoll.

Amanda was aware that Driscoll had been on the radio and given a second very poor-quality interview. It was apparent to her that Driscoll was trying to bring all of the situations under his control. The use of the Americans was supposed to strong-arm SI6 into finding a solution.

Amanda thought that in reality, Driscoll had simply added another layer of complexity. "How you getting on with our American colleagues? He asked, "I hope you have something positive to tell me by now."

"We have the two teams working together," added Amanda. "They have turned our operations room into a massive computer centre. We have enough communications to run our own TV series."

Driscoll wasn't amused. "I need something to go back to the press with," he said, "They are giving us a hard time, and I need to be able to show some results."

Amanda updated Driscoll with the news that they had tracked down a potential van that had removed Marcus from the hotel.

"So, we think we have a target group now, but we are still not sure of their background?" asked Driscoll hopefully. This would be something to tell the big chiefs.

"Well," said Amanda, "We have several people owning up to

this or at least to the bomb attacks, but we are unsure about the real origin. It can't be all of them."

Amanda had to juggle with the information back to Driscoll.

She was prepared to run the Marcus disappearance story but not that Marcus had potentially uncovered a major scheme with the Russian currency.

"Okay," said Driscoll, "You seem to have had several groups admit responsibility for the two bombs and also now you have a lead for the abduction of Marcus Barton. I call that progress, so right now I want us to mount an operation to bring down those that are claiming responsibility."

Amanda looked a little aghast.

"We are fairly certain that only one of the groups could have any claim to this. However, we don't know which one it would be at the moment."

"Look," said Driscoll, "The very fact that these groups are making claims should be enough for us to pull them in. I want us to mount an action tonight on each of these groups and to bring them into custody. It should be a combined operation. We should use our own people, the police, and the military to achieve this."

Driscoll imagined his decisiveness and leadership displayed across the media. It could work out very well for him.

Amanda realised that her work was to be cut out to do this. "What about the Americans?" She asked.

"We can't have the Americans operating in this on our soil," said Driscoll, "However I want you to use them to help you plan the campaign to bring the suspects into custody."

"We have set up the Americans as special advisers, and after the raids or whatever we need to do I would also want to feature them in our debriefs to the press. I need all of this to be actioned tonight so that it is in tomorrow morning's news. We must turn this situation around and show that we can be very proactive.

Amanda realised that she had little choice in this matter.

"If we are to do this, I will need clearance," she said. "That is clearance from the Home Office and as well as from the Ministry of Internal Affairs."

"We will get you whatever you need," said Driscoll, "You will have the necessary authorisation within another hour," he added, "It will be from me, in writing."

Amanda realised that Driscoll saw this as a fast way to get back onto the offensive over this whole situation. With Driscoll's reputation currently looking weak, this could be a way that he could turn things around for himself.

She didn't have any real option but to follow this through although she was aware that they would potentially be bringing in people that had minimal impact on the kind of events that were unfolding.

She was concerned that this was Driscoll's attempt at showmanship and that the real culprits would be would not be affected by this in any way.

Amanda decided it was better to call a short meeting with Mary-Anne and to appraise her of this. After all, if the Americans were to work with them on this, then it would be best that they knew straight away what was happening. It could also act as a massive smokescreen for the cyberattack that Daniel and the others were planning.

Amanda also realised that there was no way to run any damage limitation along with this exercise. It would be better to give it a codename and to let it all happen.

Code-word

Amanda made her way to the control room being used by the Americans. It did look like something from a spy series on television. Stacks of flat-screen monitors, twinkling lights. A glass box assembled at one end. Amanda wondered if the Americans had brought along a shop-fitting department to craft some of the environment.

"Yes, we built a quiet room too," said Mary-Anne, "A kind of anechoic chamber like the ones that recording studios use. It's the opposite of our main comms facility, designed to keep things inside."

"Okay," said Amanda, "I've something to tell you now that's top secret," she nodded towards the quiet room. "I'd like to bring Grace in as well."

"Let's go to the facility," said Mary-Anne, secretly pleased that she was able to show off just how much technology the Americans had been ready to assemble inside GCHQ.

Amanda described what Bernard Driscoll had requested. An assault on the discovered sets of suspects, despite the lack of evidence.

Mary-Anne already realised this was nothing more than a Driscoll fishing trip. That the results were likely to be slim.

"Neither you nor we have found anything substantial enough to run the kind of operation you are proposing," she said. "Unless you are not telling me something? Personally, I think this is crazy and will probably end in Driscoll being taken down like a madman. I'm not even sure that the US would want to be associated with it. We'd be seen to be interfering on foreign soil."

Amanda added, "Well Driscoll was most insistent, and it would give your co-operation the highest of profiles.

Grace added, "I doubt whether you'd walk into another NATO meeting after this without people taking notice."

Mary-Ann changed tack. "Of course, we are here to assist and support whatever you need. But. I'm not convinced that you have sufficient to go on to launch a full UK Security services and police and military intervention in your own country.

"It would be against people who are still only general suspects. We'd never be allowed to do this in the United States. It amounts to military law. You seem to have three, no four, different organisations making claims as well. There could be all kinds of ripples from this."

Mary-Anne studied the list of the groups that had laid claim to the first bomb. "Two of these are serious, but it looks to me as if the others are opportunists and/or mentally unstable."

Amanda agreed. "Yes, I've been ordered to run this with full clearance. We'll call it Operation 'Able' by the way."

"The locations we will need to visit are in London, Coventry and Berkshire. For this to work, we will need the synchronisation with several police forces as well as various army units.

"I just hope your minister knows what he is doing," said Mary-Anne, "And I will need to inform my people back in DC about this as well."

Amanda turned to Mary-Anne, "I need you to keep this very quiet," she said, "We have already had leaks related to this, and I'm worried that we will get more as extra people become aware of what is happening."

"In your case, I think we should be limiting this to the current team and perhaps your immediate controller in Washington. I've got to worry about how we do the same here in the UK."

Quietly Amanda thought that this was an excellent way for interference to be run. A distraction which would keep the Americans busy. Driscoll was still playing games to cover himself. Yet, on this occasion, he had inadvertently created something that would keep the B team very busy while Amanda's preferred A team could continue to work on the real problem.

Grace looked for the angle to test Mary-Anne.

"Of course, Mary-Anne," she said," Otherwise it will be like the leak from the American operation to setup Alya."

"What's that?" asked Mary-Anne, looking confused.

"Well, you don't think you could capture Alya in London after the Paris thing without us finding out," Grace bluffed.

"What Paris thing?"

"The Turkish Trade Minister assassination a couple of months ago. A close associate of Alexander Gulnik," said Amanda.

"Yes, Alya told us about it," continued Grace, still bluffing, "She even described you, although the name she gave was different."

Mary-Anne looked startled, "No, there's no chance of that," she replied, "I don't think America would get itself mixed up in

French matters."

"Some might say you'd not get involved in British situations either," replied Grace.

"But why don't we ask Alya directly? She's through that glass?" said Grace.

The corner of operations room into which the Americans had created their command centre had security glass in it. Not quite a one-way mirror, more the kind of glass used in supermarkets to shield the back-office from the store, while allowing those in the back office to look out.

Mary-Anne replied, "But she's seen me dozens of times."

Amanda pressed a button on her phone, "Sound now on, Alya," she said. Then irritated, she looked up, "Okay, Mary-Anne, I can see your comms retardant foam is working, let's go outside this room so that we can speak to Alya."

Outside, Alya's voice came across Amanda's phone. "It all makes more sense now. You commission me to run the job in Paris, through Pakashenko, my controller. You must have had leverage on Pakashenko- was it through Gulnik, that Turkish banker?"

Amanda added, "Alexander Gulnik was Russian, at least according to his passport."

"Well, that's curious," said Alya, "He seemed to be bankrolling Pakashenko, I thought that was why Pakashenko wanted me to run the Turkish job in Paris? As a warning to Gulnik. No one was untouchable."

"Then you get me to come to the UK to clean up behind the bombers, but really it is so that you can extract me? Exfiltrate me back to the USA? - Are the Brits in on this too, or was it a private project?"

Mary-Anne sighed.

"Go on, Mary-Anne," said Amanda, "Talk your way out of this one. I was beginning to like you, too. Now I've got your foreign asset corroborating your part in this."

"We both know that you've just bluffed enormously," said Mary-Anne,

"Not really," when we piece this together, we'll have you tied up in such a tight ball, although I'm prepared to let it slide."

"And why would you do that?" asked Mary-Anne.

"For the good of the operation. My win is that I continue unhampered. Your win is that you walk out of this undetected and with huge gold star against your name. The alternative is that you could have been found out and darkened with a big cloud. Not exactly useful for future operations."

Mary-Anne bargained," You realise you'll have to keep me in this for the ride. Otherwise, my controllers will get suspicious."

"Yeah, they'll get suspicious anyway when you drop your emergency code-word into some feedback to them," said Amanda.

"I'm afraid I'm going to have to detain you until after the operation, then to find an excuse to send you home."

Amanda used another button on her phone and immediately, a couple of armed officers walked into the operations room.

"Don't worry, we'll say you have mysteriously gone on a secret visit to Brussels, by train. That should give us time."

Raiders

"Do you know a cure for me?"

"Why yes," he said, "I know a cure for everything. Salt water."

"Salt water?" I asked him.

"Yes," he said, "in one way or the other. Sweat, or tears, or the salt sea."

— *Isak Dinesen, Seven Gothic Tales*

Raid On

Amanda's heart wasn't in the raids, but she put on her game face. They would have to follow through on Driscoll's request. She had let it be known that Mary-Anne had to make a sudden departure to Brussels, which she'd said was a cover because Mary-Anne needed to have the NATO on-side with what America was doing.

Amanda was liaising with Colonel Liddell, who would co-ordinate the battlefield dynamics of the planned situation. This was unusual, with police under the command of the military, like in a revolution or coup d'état.

Liddell was soft-spoken with a north-eastern English accent. Amanda could tell that he was tempering his words for their conversation. She imagined he'd stand for little nonsense in a conflict situation.

She advised Liddell that Mary-Anne's American team were not to be deployed. They were to stay back at the operations centre and to be used for the back-room analysis of the situation. Liddell hardly contained his pleasure on this news.

Amanda explained to Grace, " I'm sorry to have to spread this all through your estate, but I'm afraid I'm under orders from Driscoll."

Grace nodded. She knew how troublesome the Minister could be and had seen the recent television interviews.

"Look, we've got the Americans here as well, in that ops room. Now their chief has apparently gone AWOL to Brussels it leaves us with a tricky situation."

"Find out who is the second in command and insist that the Americans are very valuable doing the back-office role," said Amanda. "This situation is timetabled to run through the night. By tomorrow morning everything will have been played."

"Okay," said Grace, "But you realise this could go badly for the Minister? Armed soldiers storming civilian locations inside the UK? It's about as crazy as it gets."

"I know," said Amanda, "Don't think we haven't told Driscoll."

"Yes, but just as importantly, have you laid this off? We don't want a proverbial ton of bricks dumped at our doorstep."

"Agreed," said Amanda. "And that's why I asked Driscoll to make the command very plain. This is a direct written order from him," she waved the letter from Driscoll instructing her to conduct the raids.

Able

It was 01:00 early morning. Amanda' s own communications network was fully functioning. She had satellite video links to the four locations being raided.

The operation was to be clandestine, and the teams had been assembled as well as the creation of a 1 km perimeter around each of the targets,

The raids were set for 02:00. Amanda hoped this would be a reliable time to find the targets in bed.

Orders given to each unit were to apprehend the suspects. Retaliation was not expected but was prepared for.

The clock ticked towards 2 AM. Everyone was in position and then as 2 AM arrived, Amanda could see the operations teams moving into position led by their individual commanders.

There was a silent signal, and in each case, a series of flashing lights and muffled sounds as the teams from the tactical units deployed and surrounded the suspects.

Exceptionally, a form of tranquillizer gun was being used on all of the suspects to bring them down quickly without other injuries.

In all four cases, this worked almost immediately, and to Amanda' s surprise and relief, the four operations were over within 10 minutes of starting. By 2:30AM all of the suspects had been loaded into armoured vehicles and were being moved away towards various holding detention centres.

Liddell looked pleased. "Wow," said Grace. "Phew," said Amanda, "Now I need to call Driscoll"

For once, Driscoll also seemed pleased. He was on a video communication link to the operations centre.

He said, "I'll need my guys to be preparing the press briefing for 06:00. We need to keep a lid on this until then."

Amanda noticed that Driscoll had not said anything positive to her about the operation. He was already moving into the next phase, which was largely about covering himself in glory.

"Amanda," said Driscoll, "I guess you will want to take the initiative on the press relations for this. My main wish is that we don't give away too much about what we have done until after the various suspects have been through our interrogation processes."

Amanda nodded, "Yes, that's fine, and what are you planning to say about the American involvement with this?"

Driscoll looked directly into the camera from his end of the call, "Nothing at this time, we are not making references to the United States or their assistance".

"I'm busy now, I will talk to you again after the press and media coverage has subsided,"

Amanda nodded, "Okay, but let us know if there' s anything else we can do"

She walked out of the secure comms room and across to Grace.

"Driscoll is going to make this public tomorrow at 6 AM by his press office. I've told him not to give too much away until we have run interrogation."

Results Are In

All four of the raids had been accomplished. The sheer weight of the combined security police and military forces was pretty much guaranteed to overwhelm anyone not already prepared for some kind of military response.

Early news of those captured was also coming back to the operations room.

There was unstoppable chatter on twitter and some hand-held smartphone footage from the raids, already in syndication.

The emerging headlines were not pretty. About the gunslinging military and the heavy boot of the state. Someone had leaked the name of the operation, which also featured in some of the headlines.

'ABLE?', 'Despic-ABLE', 'UN-ABLE?', '#UnbelieveABLE'...

Amanda was also aware of the results. In the two non-London locations it was single operators running their small-time computer hacking, and as far as Amanda was concerned, these were of no real interest to the security services.

Sure, they would probably get trials and may be locked up, but really for her purposes, they were just time wasters.

The two London busts were somewhat different. In the case of the West London Hounslow situation, there had been several different individual locations raided simultaneously.

It looked as if it was a ring of people involved in something, but again Amanda was not convinced that it really had anything to do with the bombs in central London.

Potentially there was some collateral advantage in that these were dormant terrorists involved in some other caper. Still, for the purposes of this bomb threat and everything associated with the Russian currency manipulation, this was really not on the agenda.

The other south London location was similar, although the arrests were confined to a couple of houses within the same apartment complex.

The total number of people arrested was 29, and they were being kept separated from one another.

Amanda also looked at their apparent profiling and could see that they had nothing in common with one another. It was not at all likely that they were different cells from the same organisation.

It shouted Driscoll Fishing Trip and gave the services a bad name.

Maybe the individual organisations had been stupid enough to make claims about the recent bomb threats, but all this had done was unleash untrammelled force against each of them.

Amanda wondered what Driscoll would make of this in the morning for the news programmes.

In the case of the South London crew, it looked more like they were doing something with gambling and also some form of small-time industrialised forgery of name brand products. If that were the case, then this raid had probably brought in a bunch of perfume forgers. Of course, this was still beneficial to the UK as a whole but was hardly the need for such a major operation.

Driscoll was determined to put on a show in time for the early morning television and radio news broadcasts and had been working with his own PR team to get this prepared.

Amanda had provided some of the early briefings to the PR team and had tried hard to stick to the basic facts. In other words, they had arrested 29 people at four main locations, and they were suspected of being in some way connected with the bomb based upon their own claims that they had direct involvement.

Amanda knew this was face-saving speculation and hoped that the Minister would refrain from creating more confusion by drawing in these threads.

Since 5 AM the last hour of preparation had been conducted behind closed doors by Driscoll and his spin doctors.

Amanda waited for the news shows to start from around 6:30 in the morning with Driscoll's PR schedule to cover both the early morning radio and television broadcast.

At this rate, it would have blanket coverage by around 9 AM.

Of course, the newspapers would not have any of this until the following day although it would start to appear in the wire feeds and the Internet versions from probably around seven in the morning.

Technicality

Mary-Anne was still detained in a separate room in the Ops Centre.

"You'll have seen the results from the operation," asked Amanda. "I've left the TV monitoring in this room so that you are kept appraised. Grace will be joining us here, shortly."

Mary-Anne nodded," Yes, I think you've done well to get these people, but in honesty, they are not the ones you are looking for, are they?"

"I hope your minister is going to be careful about what he says," said Mary-Anne, "After all, we don't want any diplomatic incidents to arise from this, do we? For example, I understand that although the US has been involved in providing background support to this, it should remain apparent that we have not been part of your intervention team on any of the operations."

Amanda nodded. She knew that Mary-Anne would also want to distance herself from what Driscoll was about to do.

"Driscoll has decided to go his own way with this," said Amanda. "You know I will need to support him, but I'm also cautious that we don't say more than is necessary at this stage."

Driscoll's first appointment was with the Today radio programme which started at 6.30am, and Driscoll was planning to be on there from 7 o'clock in the morning. He would then have to hurry across to another studio for an interview with an early-morning BBC news programme and after that with Sky television.

Driscoll's PR had also arranged an appointment with an ITN news show so by around 8.30 in the morning he would have covered the broad spectrum.

He wanted to do this in person because he considered it such a high-profile Victory.

Grace walked into the room where Mary-Anne had been detained.

"Enjoying the facilities?" she asked, "We've tried to make this as pleasant as possible, but you understand why we've had to keep you under wraps until this operation has concluded?"

"Yes," said Mary-Anne, "We are all professionals. I'd have had to do the same if you'd been operating in the Pentagon."

"Okay, let's listen to Driscoll on the Today show."

The news was already underway as Driscoll walked into the studio. It was a small sound studio for his first interview, and he sat down at a desk by the side of a yellow coloured microphone.

He had heard the announcement in the news summarising the events of the previous evening. He recognised the wording because it had been crafted by his own marketing and press relations team.

"Welcome, Minister, you seem pleased with the outcome from the raids run last night to track down the bombers that have been detonating bombs in central London. We hear that you had four separate raids in different parts of the country. Two outside of London and two in London, one in West London and the other to the south. So, Minister, what is the latest position?

Driscoll beamed, "Yes, we believe we have caught a significant conspiracy. A total of 29 people have been arrested across the four locations, and we think they have conspired together to create the disruption to the capital.

"Each of the teams has been separately held for questioning which we are starting as this programme airs."

"Our sources, Minister, say that there is very little in common between these four groups?" said the interviewer, "For example, the two outside London are individual teenagers. One is a from a fully English background, and the other one is originally from India."

"One of the groups is said to have a large amount of counterfeit Christmas products at their location. The other group we don't yet have any further information about"

Driscoll looked slightly perplexed by this.

"No, we are in the process of tying the four groups together to show the full scale of this conspiracy. Our investigation has shown that we have unearthed a major conspiracy.

"This is a triumph for our security services and the Ministry of Internal Affairs. By using our central resources and some support from our other intelligence bureaus, we have been able to bring this to a speedy resolution."

"Minister, the opposition party, is raising questions about the way that you have deployed force to bring these people into custody," said the interviewer, "I understand that small armoured army groups were deployed each of the four sites. I'm told that there were around 40 soldiers at the each of the sites for those particular raids."

"And also, you used police force as well as the backup from other security services?"

"Of course, we did not want to take any chances with this," said Driscoll, "These are potentially all dangerous individuals."

"Minister, the opposition party says this is already beginning to smack of martial law imposed in the areas where you have provided these raids. Other people were unable to move around freely, and the sheer amount of potential firepower could have started an all-out firefight in each of the locations.

"There was intentionally a danger to other individuals that could have been greater than the effects so far from the bombing?"

Driscoll looked agitated," No," he said," That's not the case. We took the army as purely a precautionary measure to ensure that no one would escape from any of the raids that we granted."

"On whose authority were these raids co-ordinated?" asked the interviewer. "We understand it was on your direct orders that this was conducted.

"We understand that the Cobra committee is in session this morning as this broadcast goes out," said the interviewer. "It is being chaired by the Prime Minister, and there are several heads of the armed forces also involved."

"In the circumstances, did you send a representative from the Ministry of the Interior along to the Cobra session?"

Driscoll looked perplexed," I'm not aware of that meeting," said Driscoll," I assume it is part of the regular series that takes place. We normally send someone to that meeting and, yes, I do attend it myself from time to time."

"Our reporter outside the Cobra meeting place tells us that there will be a statement from Cobra this morning in at around 9 o'clock."

Driscoll again looked puzzled," I think you will find today they will want to be supporting the actions that we have taken forcefully as a deterrent and to bring the perpetrators of the London bombings into custody," he said.

Amanda, Grace and Mary-Anne were listening to the radio broadcast from the operations room.

"This is not going well," said Amanda. "I'm glad you said that." said Mary-Anne.

"Driscoll is acting unilaterally. It can't go on. Although this is a potentially bad terrorist situation with the bombs and all he can't go out with a full military force on UK soil without getting the necessary agreements first. He may consider himself above everything as the Minister of Interior but acting the way he has would create similar ripples in the United States."

Amanda nodded, "Of course, Driscoll is running on rails now through a whole series of interviews with a standard marketing pitch. I don't know whether he will try to pull out of the rest of the sessions or whether we will get some good television from watching him squirm."

"You don't seem to have a very high opinion of your minister," said Mary-Anne. "I thought it was just us, but you don't really like him. He has been quite unpleasant when he has dealt with us in the past. A very rude and arrogant man."

The radio interview had finished, and the rolling news was returning to its next iteration on the Today programme.

This time there was a feature of the interview with Driscoll at the top but the emphasis in the Today programme editorial was on the Cobra committee meeting.

"Unexpected raids on four locations involving full military presence have created a major outcry," began the news report, "An emergency meeting of Cobra has been called today to review last night's events. Minister Driscoll who was interviewed on this program this morning has admitted to running an independent operation in the small hours of this morning to round up what he describes as a major conspiracy involving four separate cells linked to the London bombing."

"He has ordered the deployment of over 200 soldiers and a similar number of police and security services across the four locations. 29 people are now held in custody from these raids which Driscoll is describing as a triumph."

"Spokesman for the opposition this morning has called this whole exercise 'the execution of military power without any prior discussion in either Parliament or a relevant subcommittee'. The Cobra committee meeting this morning chaired by the Prime Minister will issue a statement at 9 o'clock to explain the situation.

"The Today programme is being extended by 30 minutes to cover this event.

"I knew it," said Amanda," They are cancelling normal morning programs to cover this on BBC Radio Four. This is big news. Grace looked quizzically at Amanda, "What about our team and their involvement with this? There is a potential risk now from blowback."

Driscoll had already left the studio by this time. He was on his way to a small studio in the same building where he was being interviewed live for a television insert into the BBC News programme.

The media had realised that this was big news and had compressed their timeslots to ensure that Driscoll was almost seamlessly transitioned from one news studio to another.

Amanda listened to more of the reports, "I predict that within the next two hours Driscoll will be carpeted by the Cobra committee."

Amanda observed to Grace," This is an interesting turn of events, and although I could half predict it, I could not have planned this. The whole Driscoll situation provides a great diversion and cover story while we figure out what is really happening and deploy our small team of specialists."

The point

"Anyone can get a job, but do you have a purpose?"

— *Tom Butler-Bowdon, 50 Self-Help Classics*

What glory? Morning Story

Driscoll was supposed to be on his way across to the media city that generally set up opposite Parliament when anything significant was breaking.

Because of the security concerns, they had moved the media into an adjacent hotel, and he knew that there would be suites for both the ITV and Sky networks pretty much adjacent to one another.

He would be able to continue his description of the major breakthrough that he had personally supervised from these two studios.

As he walked towards the car, he was intercepted by first one of his marketing people and then by a couple of other people here did not recognise.

"Mr Driscoll," said Hannah, his PR person, "I think your sessions at the other studios have been scheduled."

Driscoll looked surprised.

"Surely not, this must be one of the biggest stories of the morning," he started,

" Yes," said Hannah, "But because of the Cobra meeting there is now a request for you to visit Cobra's location and to meet with the Prime Minister."

Driscoll looked surprised and then turned his face down towards his phone, which was displaying a significant count of messages and texts.

"What, right now?" he said, "Yes, that's right," said Hannah, "And these two people are to escort you to the Cobra location."

Driscoll could see a black Jaguar car and behind it two Land Rovers.

It looked as if he was being given a full diplomatic cavalcade to go to visit with the PM. Maybe his stakes had indeed risen.

"Okay, I guess that's what we will need to do then," he said he looked towards Jan." Are you coming along then?"

"Of course," said Hannah, "and I can brief you further in the car. There have been new developments, and we need to be on top of them. Don't say anything to anyone here."

As they walked towards the car, Driscoll sensed that not all was well.

Then Hannah started to say, "I believe the Cobra team feel somewhat left out of all of the decision-making on this. And the Labour opposition party have also registered complaints."

"They are upset because you have ordered military action without first checking with the government.

"For something like this, the Prime Minister says that he would at least be involved in the decision process.

"It has left a somewhat embarrassing situation.

"I've prepared you a few responses to some of the immediate questions raised, I have put them onto these cue cards for you, and I suggest that we spend some time in the car checking through these and agreeing which ones you think you may want to use.

"Won't be necessary," said Driscoll, "Once the PM and Cobra see that I've shut down such a major operation against the state they will the thanking me for my speedy action."

The car pulled away into the early morning traffic of central London. They would be with Cobra within another 10 minutes. Driscoll noticed that the car and a couple of forward motorcycles were using their sirens to help speed through the traffic.

Grace gestured to Amanda from within the room where Mary-Anne had been held. "We'll need to leave you now, Mary-Anne. Please call for anything that you need. We'll try to make this short stay as comfortable as possible."

Outside the room, Amanda spoke to Grace, "The Minister is on the run now, I think. I'm not altogether sure he realises it though. I doubt whether he will last the day. The Cobra committee and the Prime Minister look pretty pissed off with him about what he has been doing."

"The team here in OS12 that are running the operation with the Americans also have something that they can brag about based upon the direct orders of Driscoll, but realistically we need to focus our primary attention now on the team you have hidden away inside GCHQ. I've not breathed a word of that to the Americans.

"Will they miss you?" asked Grace," if you are away like this?"

"Normally, yes, they would, but because of the events today with Driscoll, I can easily run a camouflage set of meetings across what we are doing. It will become more obvious by tomorrow if I'm not back in business with the team in London, though."

"What else have we found out?"

"Well," said Grace," Based upon the inputs from your original London team we've been piecing together that there is some kind of currency manipulation that is being covered up by the Russians."

"The Russians have found out from the inside that your team were on to them. Then they have stopped at nothing to remove the individuals that have first-hand knowledge of the situation.

"That comprises the head of a trading group in a London bank and one of your own team - Marcus - who was writing up a paper about this.

"I think that Marcus's paper had triggered the new actions and that he was followed. I'm pretty sure that the two bombs were part of a scheme to draw Marcus out into the open."

Amanda realised that Grace had some of the story wrong and was quite pleased to think that the decoy actions were working.

Sabre-toothed kompromat

Driscoll arrived at the well-protected Sabre meeting place close to Downing Street.

He exited the car, and Hannah did so from the other side.

"You will need to wait here", someone instructed Hannah.

"Only the Minister will be allowed access to the main meeting room area."

Hannah didn't recognise the building although she could see it was one of the many of the typical central London ministry blocks.

She noticed it didn't have any signage although she could see it had a set of glass turnstiles and metal detectors through the entrance doors.

She noticed a few press, recognised one of them and sidled over.

"What's the latest?" she asked. "Hi Hannah, I should be asking you that. Do you have any story for us about Driscoll?

"We understand that he is being asked to resign," continued the news assistant. "Any comment?"

"No," said Hannah secretly knowing that the guess by the news reporter was very likely to be what was happening.

Driscoll was only inside the building for around 10 minutes.

When he emerged, he walked directly to the car that had brought him. And climbed in.

Hannah noticed he was hurrying and also ran back to get into the other side of the vehicle.

Several press people had attempted to take photographs or ask Driscoll questions, but luckily for Hannah, no one seemed to recognise her as his assistant.

The car pulled away, Driscoll's face said it all.

"So... What's the story?" asked Hannah.

" They've fired me," said Driscoll.

"They asked for my resignation. Immediately. The PM's office has given me a written statement to issue through public relations channels. Some SPAD has written it. I'm supposed to take this around to Downing Street to do it all properly. That's when they take the car back. Symbolism, don't you know?"

"I'm finished," said Driscoll, suddenly looking less intimidating than usual. "I tried to argue with them, but it was obvious they were ganging up on me. They need someone to be able to blame for what has happened, and I'm the unfortunate scapegoat."

Hannah mulled over Driscoll's recent performance and kept quiet. An excellent example of positional power being taken away from a tyrant.

"But what does this mean?" asked Hannah,

"Do I need to prepare anything to support you?"

"It doesn't look like it. I think I'm going to have to use the wording Cobra provided. The Committee seemed most insistent on it, and I don't really seem to have any other option."

"They have got, how shall we say, some other leverage which they have threatened to apply if I don't play along with this. Blasted kompromat."

Hannah could see that Driscoll was quietly seething about what had happened and still looked as if he felt he was in the right about everything. She idly wondered what else Cobra had on him.

"Turns out that they have considered three of the groups we raided were small-time. They were two teenage boys and a group of counterfeiters making perfume to sell.

"The fourth group showed some promise, but there doesn't seem to be a proper connection with the bombs in London.

"Between you and me, I was approached a few days ago by one of the aerospace manufacturers. They were offering me a role as a lobbyist and consultant. I told them to wait while I thought about it. May still do that, lots of marketing and expenses budget, as well."

"If you are taken out of the role, then who is your replacement?" asked Hannah, "and when will they start? With a major alert, there needs to be someone in place straight away."

"Bizarrely, they've given the role to SI6 as part of a holding pattern," said Driscoll, "I'm sure they will appoint a new minister but to keep things moving along Amanda Miller has been given the acting operational role directly and will be reporting into the Cobra committee."

"She doesn't know yet, but now I've been moved out of the way I expect they will be making contact with her right away."

"I guess she doesn't really have any option at the moment?" asked Jan.

"That's right," said Driscoll, "And she's already properly involved with this. I don't think the Cobra committee realises she's been working with the Americans though. That was another one of my moves to try to expedite things. Of course, we kept the American presence silent from the briefings and the press, so at the moment Amanda Miller is probably the only other person that knows."

Hannah nodded, "I guess we need to keep it that way."

"Yes, judging by what the Sabre committee did because of the military intervention, they would go even more ballistic if they knew the Americans had also been involved in the background."

Holding pattern

Amanda was considering the best course of action regarding Mary-Anne Piper. She was now, probably illegally, holding a US-Citizen inside the greater GCHQ complex.

Mary-Anne's external credentials would doubtless show as something innocuous like an office worker, which designed to give the maximum sympathy vote if she was ever detained.

She could probably get Mary-Anne held now on various charges related to the bombing, but this would also create a major international incident, and she didn't want to be responsible for the US blacklisting the UK.

She would have to see how it played out if she approached Mary-Anne directly about options.

Mary-Anne had a few of her own too.

"You know this is illegal," Mary-Anne said, "You may have only held me for a day, but as this unrolls you are getting yourself in deep."

"Mary-Anne, we could make this whole bombing incident go away," said Amanda," But you'll need to give us something in return. Two parts: Firstly, you'll provide us with ongoing information,"

"What, a double agent," said Mary-Anne, she laughed, "Think very carefully when you ask for something like that!"

"It doesn't have to be very much," said Amanda, "Just a sign of co-operation. I'm offering you a way off the hook here. Probably a chance to walk out with some credit."

Mary-Anne stiffened in the chair, "Keep talking," she said.

"So secondly, I'll want an address."

"Address?" asked Mary-Anne, "For what?"

"We want to get Marcus Barton back," said Amanda, "We know you are holding him."

Mary-Anne paused. Amanda could see she was weighing up options.

"All right," said Mary-Anne, "but you will have to let me go now. It will look more obvious, the longer you keep me in detention.

"Let me go, and I'll do two things. First, give you the address for Marcus and second, when the time is right, I'll do some extracurricular work. Understand that the second offer will be time-limited. Use it or lose it."

"We'll get this agreement drafted," said Amanda, amazed that the negotiation had worked. Mary-Anne must have realised she had run out of road, "You'll have to give me the address now. A sign of good intention."

Mary-Anne considered again. "Okay, I'll need to have been released within two hours."

"You have my word, subject to you signing our agreement," said Amanda, amused that Mary-Anne was already trying to gain higher ground.

Chain

"You show the world as a complete, unbroken chain, an eternal chain, linked together by cause and effect."

— *Hermann Hesse, Siddhartha*

Safe House

Marcus had been in the safe house now for several days. It didn't seem very Russian to him; in fact, it seemed more as if the Americans had taken him.

On the second day, he'd been approached by one who had asked him to co-operate on the foreign exchange theory. These captors seemed to know less about it than he did. He didn't want to be giving them more than necessary.

Marcus tried to remember his training from back in the days when he had started working at C-SOC. He recalled that the threat of torture was often as good as its actual conduct. He wondered why there had been no explicit moves in that direction; after all, he had been tranquillised and bundled into a laundry van.

Considering all things, they had been looking after him reasonably well. He couldn't work out where he was except that it was still in the UK. He could see out of the window and had worked out that there were significant contrails from planes overhead.

His guess was he was on the flight path to one or other of the big London airports, but he couldn't guess which one.

The house was a neutral semi-detached house. He assumed the

other half was filled with 'operatives' of whatever this group represented.

The windows were armoured glass and also had security bolts. The doors were all locked. As people moved through the house, there seemed to be a key protocol to get from one area to another.

There were various comings and goings too. Marcus assumed it was a shift change. He had seen a wide range of different people. There didn't seem to be anyone in charge, but they all seemed to know about him and that they needed to hold him.

Then, one day, there was a knock on the door. He saw several people moving swiftly. "It's Mary-Anne," he heard on the speakerphone.

One of the guards moved to open the door. A woman stepped in. Marcus didn't recognise her. Then, two other women. He recognised one of them.

"He is over there," said the guard, pointing towards Marcus.

"This is one of the weirdest handovers I've ever been involved with," the guard said to Mary-Anne.

"We'll need this to stay off the books too," said Mary-Anne. "The matter is quite delicate."

Rosie nodded to the other woman that had entered behind Mary-Anne.

"Yes, it's him,"

Marcus realised that Rosie had been brought along for identification. He kept a stony face, as the training had taught him. "Don't show recognition; it might be a trap."

Mary-Anne beckoned to Marcus,

"You'd better come over here now," we are taking you to a debriefing point.

Marcus moved slowly towards the three women. He could see more people outside the front door of the house. They had the bearing of military but were dressed in casual clothes. He glimpsed a red van standing at the kerbside.

"Yes, you're going in that," said Mary-Anne. Royal Mail.

Marcus walked outside. He could feel his heart racing. What if this suddenly got nasty?

He could hear the other women speaking to Mary-Anne," You've got two hours to clear this down. Then I'm sending in people to look it over."

Mary-Anne nodded. She realised she had just dodged a significant career misfortune.

Outside in the Royal Mail van, Marcus waited for Rosie to appear.

"I wondered if you'd make much as a field agent," said Rosie, "But I think you are much too valuable."

"And this is who you have to thank for this non-violent escape plan," said Rosie, indicating Amanda," and to be honest we wondered if you were still alive."

"Can we talk freely?" asked Marcus.

"Yes, it's fine," said Amanda, "I'm from GCHQ. Amanda Miller."

"I've been out of it," said Marcus. "They didn't seem to know so much and kept asking me about C-SOC. I'm not sure if they knew why they were holding me."

"It was a safe house. I expect they were the hired help."

"They seemed to be Americans, rather than Russians," said Marcus.

"Yes, they were Americans. You may have been extracted by a Russian, but the people holding you were Americans."

"That explains a lot," said Marcus, "I was having trouble piecing it together."

"So, what have we discovered?" He asked. Rosie leaned towards him and began to explain.

Embassy Chain

Daniel, Kyle and Matt had been locked away in the operations planning room. It had become a mess of discarded food and drinks.

"It's not like the old days with cardboard pizza boxes and plastic cups," mused Tyler.

Matt and Drew nodded. "No, we're a green site nowadays," agreed Daniel, "Although it was mad when they were sending out the paper circulars to remind everyone."

Kyle looked at the whiteboard, "So somehow the Russian Central Bank is shoring up the Rouble? It seems to be through a cyber currency, but somehow the Russians are masking its use."

"They seem to be doing this from many countries too," added Daniel.

"Yes," said Tyler," the countries seem to correlate with territories where Russia has an Embassy or a Trade delegation."

Kyle added, "That is very similar to the idea that Matt had. But because he was a self-financing student, he never had a chance to put the grand scheme into practice. But I suppose someone else could?"

Matt said," The very basis of cyber currency is the sophisticated number mining that is required to generate new money. The whole purpose is to stop cheats from being able to forge the connections that make up the blockchain used for trading the values. The Americans asked me to support them because my discovery system was faster than anything they could make themselves. All just based upon my algebra addition."

"Now Russia seem to have adopted the same idea to build a closed-loop system that looks realistic. Heaven help anyone who joins it. I guess they stole the concept from the Americans."

"But to do it on a distributed industrial scale would require an immense amount of computing power in the first place," said Daniel.

"That's right," said Kyle, "you'd need to be some multinational giant to do this particularly as you need to keep the whole chain under your control without anyone else being able to add anything to it."

"Could a major international power do this?" Asked Daniel

"Yes, I wondered whether a corporation could do it first," said Kyle, "The challenge is to have ways to be able to ship some of it around in a hidden format to create the initial building blocks. With all the government regulations for most types of international messaging traffic, this would be almost impossible."

"Unless maybe you're a government in your own right? And maybe have also got some diplomatic channels available?" asked Daniel.

Kyle nodded, "Yes, I suppose that Russia could attempt to do this. It would still be pretty difficult, and they'd need an awful lot of computing power which should ideally be stashed away in different countries too,"

"Not necessarily a problem; Russia has embassies all over the world," added Tyler.

"It also has both secure comms networks and satellite channels," said Kyle.

"Perhaps we can look at unusually large computer centres being used by the Russians in their embassies?" said Tyler.

"If they have any sense, they will have put them somewhere else," said Kyle," In other words not inside the embassies but in some other place where they can run an ostensibly conventional business under Russian ownership."

"Maybe," said Daniel, "but that adds another leak point to the system. If what you're describing here is true and they have figured out how to do this, then they are in effect simply printing money in a way that is almost undetectable to anyone else. In anyone's hands, this is a huge weapon. I'd keep it locked down."

"Right," said Tyler," So now we need to design a virus that can penetrate Russian embassies around the world. Easy peasy."

"Ahem," said Daniel, "there is a little something that we've been working on over the years that could do that kind of thing."

Disrupter

"So, now we are trying to hack into the Russian Federation's main embassy systems? And also across into the financial world?" asked Tyler.

"We'll need to devise a trojan horse to get into the Russian Embassy systems. A couple of options would be through the financial services systems or the taxation systems?" said Daniel.

"They are both pretty good ideas," said Kyle, "but I think they will be heavily firewall and virus-checked. We might need something less obvious."

"Let's see; the Embassy knows information about people. What about if they received the payload via the people tracking system?" said Daniel, "It's a lot more rudimentary than the other systems and probably less well protected. That's pretty much the basis of our little prototype system."

Daniel walked across to a whiteboard and wrote two words on it: passports and credit cards. "

What do both of these things have nowadays?" asked Daniel - "they both contain microchips. We could introduce the payload into the microchips that are included in regular passports or as a way to hack into the Russian Embassy and Consulate systems.

"We could expand their electronic wallets and use them to inject the payload, which will eventually need to find its way across to the banking system."

"This will only work if we do it on a fairly wide scale so that we are able to seed the payload in various different locations."

Daniel started, "We've already built the injector software for this, but it's an altogether different story to get it set up into passports and credit cards."

Kyle chipped in, "Yes, a small app on the passport runs a loader for a bigger payload. The bigger payload is the real app that can deliver the currency swap-over.

Chris nodded and looked quite excited with Daniel's suggestion. "You know something; I think this could work. It would be the way to get the initial code into the system at several different locations. The payload code would be something we could send in separately once we had seeded smaller applications to provide the priming for the receipt of the main code.

He started to draw a diagram, "See, it's a bit like a drill for a big hole where you have two drill a small pilot hole first. The pilot hole is the small payload on the passport and then the main item is delivered separately.

"How many passports do we issue per week?" asked Grace.

"It's about 5-6million per year, so probably around 250,000 per week," said Amanda.

"That should start the spread of the virus nicely," said Kyle.

"The payload itself is easier. Once an Embassy has the virus, it can request the rest of the software."

'Pull, rather than Push," said Tyler.

"Exactly, we get the embassies to request their own updates, complete with the blockchain disrupter.'

"Great," said Kyle," The other thing we must consider is how to make the whole thing look untraceable."

"Well, we'll host the disrupter software from several foreign sites. We'll add in some Cyrillic code and maybe some Chinese as well, it doesn't have to do anything, except look realistic," said Daniel.

Going viral

Amanda could see that Matt, Daniel and Kyle had been busy.

With the mixture of Daniel's Embassy cracker, the 'bought from the internet' virus kit and Matt's seed key calculator, they now had a test rig created.

They had designed a small virus which could start a collapse of the blockchains.

"It works by moving the blockchain to another 'universe,'" explained Kyle to Amanda.

"Imagine the fully intact blockchains that have been seeded by one of Matt's unique keys. Matt changes the key, and the blockchain segment moves. By changing all of the blockchain keys, we will move all of the blockchains. They will still show integrity, but there will be no way to access them, except with the revised key."

"It's a great idea," said Amanda, "but how will the system be seeded to start this process??'

We needed to get around the usual Embassy protection software, so we did what most hackers do and looked for the outer extremities. It led us to, wait for it, the border.

"What Border control?" asked Amanda.

"Precisely," said Daniel, "It focuses on the physical rather than the digital and is a weak point."

"We are planning to revamp the code in UK Citizen passports. To make them into the equivalent of uploadable viruses. Then, when the Russians scan the passports, they will start the process to infect their embassy computers."

"Won't this also work for other countries?" asked Amanda.

"No," answered Kyle, "We've added the Russian Country code prefix into the validity test."

"What's that?" asked Amanda.

"Er it's 007," said Kyle sheepishly, "Double O 7?" replied Amanda, "You are not making that up?"

"I know, it kills me to say so, but it is true," answered Tyler.

"Okay so the virus uploads after checking the country code, then what?"

"It is a lightweight virus and, when activated, uploads the separate payload code, which will change the blockchain values."

"From where does it get it? Not GCHQ, I hope?"

"Well, we are intercepting passports at the point of issue, it uses the original technique we designed for the Olympics, high speed re-encoding" said Daniel.

"And we are spreading the main payload around the internet at the moment. Chinese, Russian, American, Scottish, Dutch, Israeli sites and some of them even mirror to other countries."

"Good, so we are trying to cover our tracks?"

"Yes," said Daniel," And the new passports come with an anti-tamper addition. Try to tamper with them and the firmware breaks. We won't publicise that, of course,"

"Okay, so who do we need to alert to all of this?"

"I think, Amanda, it is you, now that the minister has handed over control."

"In fairness, I think this government-sponsored retaliation to a government-sponsored cyber-attack is wholly justified."

"Especially if we don't get caught," said Tyler.

Amanda looked across to Grace and sighed," Well, we'd better get on with it then."

Cleanup

Matt was highly organised. He had worked with Daniel to commandeer the main control room in OS12. This had meant the removal of several of the American Team, who Grace had provided with a 'special facility' inside the main GCHQ complex.

It had worked, she was delighted to see the Americans setting up various types of probe and monitoring device all of which had been connected to a sports TV network and was providing them with harmless information about Rugby and an international athletics event.

Matt had set up a range of large monitors, added a map of the world and was getting ready to track the various newly seeded passports as they appeared on Russian soil.

The maps showed a few solitary yellow lights depicting new passport holders arriving in Russian locations.

"Softly, softly," said Kyle as he watched the display. A single light turned to green.

"It's picked up the virus."

"Where is that?"

It's St Petersburg, the Summer Garden, answered Matt. We're into the first Russian government building and have uploaded the virus.

Another light went green.

"Petrozavodsk," said Matt. "This one is in a bank, Sberbank Rossil,"

Tyler watched the map. Moscow suddenly appeared with a selection of red lights.

"A plane has arrived, they are new passengers clearing the security,"

Another lone red marker, far to the east. "Yuzhno-Sakhalinsk", on the island of Sakhalin. "That's an oil-town," said Daniel.

"We're getting some decent coverage," said Kyle.

"Look," said Matt. Several more of the reds had turned to green. The virus has been successfully uploaded a few more times.

"Krasnoyarsk," said Matt, "the planes have been busy."

"I don't even know where half of these places are," said Kyle. Tyler nodded agreement.

"Well, some of these places are really the receiving ends for banking and financial transactions," said Daniel.

"The more interesting one is still Moscow. The bigger embassies and banks will have satellite arrays to bounce their signals to the far corners of the Russian Federation."

"Let us wait to see how that proliferates."

Daniel pointed to the map. New York was lit up, "Russian Embassy, in New York," he said.

A few more red lights appeared on the map. Then Paris, and Berlin.

"It has started," said Kyle,

Daniel Nodded.

"Yes, let's hope they don't notice!"

Amanda asked," How long have we got?"

~Daniel looked around from the map.

"The rate it is going, we've got about thirty minutes before we have enough spots to guarantee good coverage."

"The virus will automatically load the 'payload program', which is what we need to execute the code. To run the 'exploit'."

"Exploit?" asked Amanda.

"Yes, we will trigger the application that will move the blockchains. That's when they will start to notice something; we'll be able to set things up quietly before that."

Matt looked at the map.

"We have a problem," he said.

"Take a look at this," He pointed to a particular cluster of dots, most of which had turned green.

A few were now yellow.

"What does yellow mean?" Asked Amanda.

"It means they have been detected," said Matt. "There must be some kind of Malware detection in those sites. They are neutralising our virus."

Matt looked across the map. There were, by now, many red dots and a significant and increasing number of green dots.

"A few yellow dots had appeared in a diagonal swathe, east of Moscow.

"It's the Urals," said Matt, "they are a separate time zone and must have particularly good security software installed."

Sure enough, the areas around Ekaterinburg, Perm and Salekhard were all switching from green to yellow. The virus was being contained.

Matt looked at Kyle, "Its borderline whether we have enough locations seeded yet," he said as he looked across to Daniel.

"We've got to let it go, or we risk Urals alerting the adjacent zones to the problem. If that happens and Moscow is contained, then we'll reduce our chance to be successful even more."

Kyle nodded. "Matt, we've gotta let this thing loose."

Matt also nodded and began typing into a console.

"Okay, here we go, I'm letting the blockchain mover loose."

A screen to the right of the maps showed the Rouble to dollars position.

"It's holding steady," said Kyle. Then, a small movement downward.

" I think that could be it," said Kyle. Daniel nodded. Amanda looked on, waiting for more of an explanation.

"We can see the rouble weakening. Russia doesn't appear to have as much foreign exchange as it thought. The cyber currency is no longer in play. They can see that it is trickling away, but it will look like a software bug that has caused it."

"The Americans will be delighted," said Amanda to Grace. "This is their idea of economic warfare."

"Well, if the Russians had not tried it first," said Grace, "then none of this would be happening."

Kyle looked at Matt. If only they knew, how this had all started with the Americans.

And now the Americans were pretty much getting what they wanted.

Market shifts

"Hello, this is BBC News.

"An unprecedented rush on foreign exchange markets occurred today. It has left some currencies reeling, with others attempting to match their positions as a result of national bank interventions.

"The Bank of England has said it is not involved in any form of Quantitive Easing and that the inherent strength of the GBP will allow it to hold its position.

"The US dollar has also been under pressure today, but because of US reserves, it has been able to hold steady.

"The most significant impact today has been on Russia, who stated that their stock of foreign currency had depleted.

"A Russian spokesperson has indicated that there are allegations of economic manipulation of the currency markets targeting the rouble.

"Sources indicate that the Euro is also holding steady…"

Tyler looked towards the TV.

"They would say that, wouldn't they? And after all, they can't come on too strong because of the manipulation that they have been running.

"Agreed, answered Kyle, "This is an interesting situation now, although we've accidentally tipped this back to a US advantage."

"Not exactly," said Matt, "Don't tell anyone yet, but those passports might just be programmed with a second country code."

Palmer Street

"Come on then," said Tyler, "I think a small celebration is in order. Marcus is back, and we've neutralised the money printing. We've caught the Russian agent and discovered that the Americans can be quite tricky. And Amanda is the new chief! Where, in Cheltenham, do GCHQ types go drinking? " asked Tyler.

"Tradition was to go Palmer Street," said Daniel, "Except it doesn't exist any more."

"What's Palmer Street?"

"The old GCHQ headquarters before we built the doughnut," said Daniel.

"The nearest pub to Palmer Street is probably the Wetherspoons in the town centre."

"Well, in that case, we'll just have to improvise," said Tyler,

"Bottle of Sauce, then?" suggested Daniel.

"Huh?" Asked Tyler.

"It's nearby, and we'll get a table," said Daniel.

They arrived at the pub. It was painted an all-over grey, much in the style of Starbucks with their all-black look. The group of them crashed inside, and Rosie headed for a large round table.

"Drinks all round?" asked Kyle, taking note of the individual requests and then heading to the bar with Tyler.

"Like the olden days," he quipped.

They returned to the table with a laden tray of drinks.

"So, go on then," said Rosie, "I doubt we'll ever get another chance to hear about the student flat."

"Yes, we lived in a flat in London, Kensington actually. We were all mathematicians and somehow seemed to be able to edit out the squalor of our surroundings."

"I was studying physics," said Kyle, "In case you forgot."

"Then Matt invented the cyber thingy, and we all got sucked into this!"

Rosie smiled, "You really were a collection of propeller heads in that flat!"

"We were, as the chicken said to the pig, 'committed to breakfast', by this time though, We'd blown a term's money on the hardware that Matt bought and which I paid him half towards and the only way we expected to recoup our costs was to find some of these new blockchain hashes, "said Tyler.

"Yes, and that's about when we were recruited by C-SOC," said Tyler, "I'd been able to exchange the early finds from Matt through the banking built into the gambling sites, but it became too high a traffic volume and likely to raise suspicion. Me paying in one amount, running a few gambles and then pulling all the money out again was beginning to look suspicious."

Tyler's phone rang.

"Hello," he said, "It must be another job offer! Excuse me," he said as he walked to the door of the pub.

"Erica?... I wasn't expecting you!"

"Hi, Tyler, something you should know. I think I've just heard from Victor. It came through as a text, and from a weird phone as well. I've just sent it through to you, as well."

As she was speaking, a text pinged through to Tyler's phone.

"Trouble with rissia means I've hidden since STP with Drew. Friday@sameplace. V"

"Okay," said Tyler," I'm not sure I get it."

"Rissia - a standing joke between Drew and Victor, who can't text message very well. STP - refers to the meal that Victor had with Drew and the location."

"STP usually means sticky toffee pudding?" joked Tyler.

"Yes, You boys, and what's a Rules Speciality? - the STP, so Victor is signalling to be met at Rules on Friday."

Lost and Found

"There are so many ways to go wrong.
All we've got are metaphors, and they're never exactly right.
You can never just
Say. The. Thing."

—*Jennifer Egan, A Visit from the Goon Squad*

Rules

Tyler and Erica arrived at Rules, the restaurant that Victor had indicated. They were early and had also asked Matt and Amanda to take up a second table reasonably close to where they would meet.

Sure enough, at 5pm, Victor entered the restaurant. Erica and Drew looked surprised to see Victor, who was bearded and wearing some large rimmed glasses.

"Victor, we thought you'd been abducted, or even worse," said Erica.

"Yes, I had to disappear; I'm still in hiding, these people don't mess around."

"So, what has been happening then? "asked Erica." We've found out about the cybercash, the laundering and the Russian takeover."

"Yes, that's when it all went to shit," said Victor. "I was asked by US sources to run this laundering and to keep it below the radar. I set up with the KIV Bank for the money to be washed, but the Russians worked out what was happening.

"They sent Alexander Pakashenko to threaten me. I'd been helping some American friends with connections to move money, but the FBI was not so interested because they could see it was damaging to the rouble.

"American friends with connections? you mean the Mafia?" asked Erica.

"Yes, although I don't think they call themselves that anymore. It attracts too much attention."

"You idiot," said Drew, "Did you ever expect to get out from under that? And you tried to drag me into it too!"

"I know," said Victor, "The situation ran away from me. The CIA discovered me, but instead of hauling me in, they asked me to continue. They were more interested in the economic turmoil that could be created by issuing extra money. They were trying to run a kind of economic sanction against the Russian Federation. I was in the firing line for Corporate fraud.

"That's when Pakashenko threatened me. He said I should flip sides to help the Russians directly. He introduced me to another Russian, Alexander Gulnik, who seemed to be so cash-rich it was unbelievable."

"But we think Pakashenko was playing both sides, in any case," said Tyler.

"But if they find you now?" asked Erica, "then what?"

"Bang, I think. I need witness protection to get out from this. I've managed to hide away until today, but I don't fancy my chances going forward. I was told that there is a female assassin after me now, in any case."

"I think we may be holding her", said Tyler. "She seems to have been brought over for multiple purposes. She was being directed by Pakashenko."

"Well, I think I've told you what I know," said Victor, "And I'm looking for a trade. My silence about all of this in return for a placement package."

"I take it you have money already?" asked Erica.

"Yes, I have plenty of cash hidden away. I need to disappear completely somehow, so that I can get on with my life."

"I'll need to introduce you to someone," said Tyler, gesturing to Amanda.

"Yes, we can assist you," she said, "but you'll have to turn state witness first, to put on record what has been happening. We don't intend to use it because we've been up to a few tricks of our own, but it will be useful to have the situation, and the participants filed away."

"I will cooperate," said Victor. "So long as you can get me out of this."

Russian advances

It was a quiet runway on an airstrip in Kent.

Mary-Anne stepped from the car.

"Good to see you again," she said to Amanda, "I've no idea how this has turned out, you've kept me in radio silence for the last two weeks."

"Yes, things have moved fast, you'll have to promise not to divulge any of this though. If you do, then I'm afraid it will bite you too."

"Say we are incompetent. Say you needed to guide us through this, that our minister was a loose cannon. You can say what you like but stay away from what really happened in Cheltenham."

"Yes, you were there, you met us and decided we were underpowered. Say that your setting up of the big communication room was our only hope. But that it didn't find anything. They've packed their equipment away again and are on their way back to Heathrow Cargo terminal.

"You'll be on a flight from here to Frankfurt. Ah yes, and why did you go to Brussels? To clear up what you thought was a manipulation of the Euro against the dollar.

"Here. Here are the meeting notes from the sessions you

attended."

Amanda handed over a set of papers, neatly filed into a slim binder.

"How?" asked Mary-Anne, surprised that GCHQ had done so much to give her an alibi.

"Oh, don't worry, we sent someone along. She was a pretty good facsimile of you. Just a little more - how would we say - European. I think you'll have done wonders for US-EU relations. Now it's time to put this all back in the box. That includes Victor Boyd."

"Boyd? The banker?"

"Yes, Boyd, who has been helping 'organised crime' to launder money."

"You knew?" Asked Mary-Anne.

Of course, we knew, how else could the CIA put the screws onto Victor, except by pretending to be criminal masterminds. Bringing in your fake Russian Pakashenko worked for both Boyd and Alya. You have certainly scared Victor Boyd enough. He won't be saying anything to anyone.

"That's my point," said Mary Anne, "We don't need anyone breaking ranks on this."

They walked the few paces towards the steps on the small jet.

"I'll wish you a pleasant flight. You're heading for Frankfurt and then back to the US on Lufthansa. It's a very European return flight."

Mary-Anne smiled. "You are so - European," she said to Amanda.

"I know," said Amanda, "I'll take that as a compliment."

Roundup

Matt, Kyle and Tyler sat together in the pub.

"Hey - this is becoming a habit like it was back in the day," said Kyle.

"Except we all know a bit more now," said Matt.

"At least my theory about multi-threading the blockchains worked, the Russians managed to prove that," said Matt.

"And a couple of us are still in a job," said Tyler, "And Kyle, you've even managed to land some contracts with the security services."

"And we've made a few interesting contacts along the way," said Kyle.

Yes, and we've managed to wreak havoc on a global scale. The Russians are re-negotiating their pipeline deals with Turkey again.

"The Americans will think twice before they try stealth-based economic tactics," said Tyler.

"...And Erica's shitty boss Victor has disappeared, as, indeed, has Driscoll from the Ministry. It's much better to have

Amanda there."

"Although I see Bernard Driscoll has turned up working for one of the big defence contractors, nothing like a good Teflon coating," said Kyle.

"But Matt, I've still got a question for you," said Kyle.

"When the virus changed all those blockchains around; surely someone still has access to them? That's an awful lot of cybercash magic'd into infinity?"

"Maybe…" said Matt, "But THAT would be telling!"

Ingram Content Group UK Ltd.
Milton Keynes UK
UKHW020358090323
418239UK00015B/1158